MURDER AT THE SEASIDE

BRIAN GEE

BLOODHOUND
— BOOKS —

www.bloodhoundbooks.com

Print ISBN 978-1-914614-81-1

For Tracy
Thank you for all of your love and support

CHAPTER ONE

W hat was that noise?

There it went again, a strange buzzing that cut through his dream. As he opened his eyes, he saw that a light was flashing on and off in the bedroom.

In that time that seems to take forever but which lasts only microseconds, Crofts realised it was his phone vibrating on the wooden bedside table, and the strange lights weren't in fact an alien spaceship but also from the phone. Crofts glanced at the screen; it was a private caller, which could mean only one thing: work. It was twelve minutes past three in the morning.

'Good morning, Mr Crofts, this is the control room. Sorry to bother you,' said a cheery voice.

Why do the controllers always say that? mused Crofts, knowing this was someone wide awake and halfway through their shift.

'I've been asked to call you by the on-call SIO, as we have a suspicious death over in Hastings. Do you want me to tell you about it now, or do you want to wake up properly and get back to me?'

'I'll get back to you,' said Crofts. He knew that any further conversation whilst lying in bed would wake up his wife, Deborah, and maybe even his young son, Oscar, who was asleep in the next room. Much better to wake up properly to get the information. Anyway, if a senior investigating officer from the major crime team was involved, it would be something that needed more than a quick chat.

Crofts got out of bed quickly and was wide awake before he got to the spare room. Years of conversations in the middle of the night had made sure he was quickly alert, as any decisions made during those first few moments could be crucial to the investigation. Being half asleep was no excuse for mistakes in this line of work.

Crofts called the control room back. This controller was just as cheerful. *He has probably just finished his break; sounds like he's been filling up on some M&M's or Cherry Coke,* thought Crofts.

'Hi, Simon, what we have is a suspicious death over in Hastings,' said the happy controller, as if he were telling him he had won the lottery.

Crofts muttered 'What a surprise' under his breath. Having covered Hastings for fifteen years, he had got used to the lifestyle of some of its inhabitants, and it wasn't what the tourists to the area imagined. His version of Hastings included drugs and squalor, together with a less desirable type of foreign visitor. This influenced most of the crime in the town, and it hadn't improved even though the local authorities had tried to inject cash into the place.

'Any other details at this time?' asked Crofts.

'It appears that it involves some druggies who have been living in a squat,' continued the happy one. 'They've had a binge and woke up to find one of them is dead. Someone phoned it in but fled the scene. Ambulance attended, but the crew aren't happy with some of the injuries to the body.'

'Okay,' said Crofts. 'I'll start heading over. Who's the on-call SIO?'

'It's Tom Mead. But there's one other thing.'

'Which is?'

'There's no lighting inside the squat and there are holes in some of the floors.'

'In that case, I don't want anyone else to enter that building until I get there,' Crofts replied. 'I need to assess the scene before we decide what to do next. Have you called a SOCO yet?'

'Yes, it's Hannah Jukes. She's on her way from Eastbourne too.'

Crofts had a quick wash and cleaned his teeth, his mind working on the information he had been given so far. The fact that it was a suspicious death with some type of drugs connection made things easier. It wasn't going to be a Category A type of murder, where the offender was unknown to the victim. At some stage the two had been together in this type of murder, and it would cut down the amount of work they would need to do at the scene. The dangers of a squat inhabited by drug users were a whole different kettle of fish. Over the years he had learnt that anything could be around in these types of places. Used needles, drugs and all the paraphernalia that went with them. And if there was no electricity and holes in the floors, that just added to the mix.

Coupled with those problems was the fact that the inhabitants of these places didn't exactly live a clean lifestyle. No washing, no changing of clothing and quite often faeces, both humans' and dogs', all over the place. 'Lovely,' Crofts muttered to himself as he went into the kitchen to boil the kettle. His house seemed like a show home compared to where he was heading, even though Deborah always worried about it being untidy. He'd lost count of the number of times he'd said he would like to take her round some of the hovels he had to work in to show her how clean their home really was.

Crofts always made himself a cup of tea before setting off at this time of day, as you never knew when you would get another cuppa. While he waited for the kettle to boil, he called Hannah. She was just heading out to her van to drive over to Hastings. Crofts told her of his decision that no one was to enter the building until he arrived and he could hear the relief in her voice. Although she had been a SOCO for about three years, Hannah still needed reassurance sometimes, especially on a more complicated scene like this.

He remembered that he was like that when he first started, but after fifteen years in the scenes-of-crime world there wasn't much that fazed him anymore.

Most police forces had changed to calling their investigators CSIs due to the popularity of the American TV series, but in Sussex they were glad they had remained scenes-of-crime officers or SOCOs. Now they were all civilian staff, unlike when Crofts had joined when half the numbers were police officers. To begin with, there had been the worry that civilians couldn't carry out the role properly, but this was unfounded. Crofts and his fellow senior SOCOs were held in great esteem, especially by the major crime teams, who relied on their evidence to convict the bad guys.

Crofts finished his tea, grabbed his blue investigator's notebook and headed out to the Ford Focus Estate he used when on call. As usual, he marvelled at the stillness of the night outside. It was the best part of the day. No noise, no one around, peace and calm before the dawn broke. As Crofts opened the car door, he hoped that he wouldn't wake any of his neighbours when he started the engine. He lived in a quiet close near the

Sovereign Harbour and got on well with those who lived around him. They always said they didn't hear him in the night, but he was never too sure.

He drove out of the residential area and on to the A259, towards the wonders of Hastings.

CHAPTER TWO

Only two miles away someone else was also awake, but in her case, Bethany knew exactly what it was that had interrupted her sleep. It was the idiot upstairs, who was having another one of his 'gatherings'.

He had told her before that he didn't have parties, just gatherings. Parties were much louder and would involve more people. But as usual, the gathering seemed to be getting louder and louder, just as Bethany was trying to get to sleep. She had finished a twelve-hour shift as a waitress that evening and had another in the morning, so sleep was all she wanted now. It was impossible. She could hear almost every part of the drunken conversations that interspersed the music, the walls were that thin.

She longed to get away from here – she hated it. Not long now, she told herself. Only a few more weeks and she would have saved enough to get a flat of her own and leave this awful place. It was called the Foyer – a trendy kind of name for a place where teenagers and young adults lived. The idea behind it was good: a warden-controlled haven for young people with problems or without any family.

Since Bethany had been in care most of her life, when she became too old to be fostered, this was always where she was going to end up.

All those memories of lovely times with foster families, in between menacing council-run children's homes had made her more determined than others to get out of here and live on her own, in her own place, for the first time in her life.

Her mother had been a heroin addict and a prostitute who had never wanted a child. She hadn't known who Bethany's father was, as it could have been any of the many clients she'd serviced to enable her to afford her habit.

Her pregnancy had been good; she'd found out that lots of punters liked being with a pregnant woman, and in fact some had asked for her by name for that reason. But after the birth, none of them had been interested.

When she had realised that she wouldn't be able to work as she had before, meaning she wouldn't be able to afford heroin, Bethany's mother had turned against her. Luckily, social services had been aware of the problem and had got Bethany away from that environment to safety. No one knew if her mother had realised what was happening, as she had probably been too stoned to understand, and too stoned to care.

Within a year she was dead from a heroin overdose on a batch of bad gear that also took the lives of two of her friends before word got around that it was dangerous. Only a couple of people had attended the funeral. Bethany hadn't been one of them.

So here Bethany was, in the Foyer, unable to sleep. She couldn't go and complain to the neighbours as she had no make-up on and they would laugh at her.

Bethany was small and petite – some would say pretty – but her most prominent features were her large brown eyes. When she was younger, she had been ridiculed for looking like a meerkat. This wasn't helped by the fact that at that time an insurance company had used meerkats in their advertising. Bethany had cried nearly every night in that home as the merciless bullies constantly teased her about it.

As she grew older, she had learnt to use make-up to disguise her eyes so that they were now an asset to her appearance. She also dyed her hair black. The effect was an attractive, mysterious look that she could hide behind, and that was how everyone knew her now. Letting anyone see her without make-up was a definite no-no.

She decided to count in her head how much money she had saved so far to try to get to sleep. She had been working at The Moorings for six months and couldn't believe how lucky she was.

When she was fourteen, she had been fostered by a lovely couple who ran a local pub. Not only was it a safe environment for her, but it had also introduced her to the life of a publican's family. It was hard work but great for socialising. Bethany met lots of new people, which brought her out of her shell. She was also able to help with all the varied tasks in the pub and eventually, when she was old enough, she worked behind the bar, which she loved. It meant she was able to get a job at any pub or restaurant, as she knew the trade inside out, and when she decided that the hair and beauty course at college was a waste of time, she returned to bar work, as she had realised it was what she wanted to do.

She could have gone back to The King's Arms, but everyone knew her background, so she looked elsewhere. An acquaintance from college – she didn't have any actual friends – had told her about The Moorings. It was a pub-cum-restaurant on the beach at nearby Pevensey Bay run by a couple, Malcolm and Sandy, and had a good name for value-for-money food –

'Three courses for a tenner' was their motto. It meant that it was always busy and needed hard-working, reliable staff.

Bethany had gone along for a trial, and Sandy had been so impressed she had started that night. It wasn't the best wages going, but as Bethany had no other commitments, she could work as many hours as needed, and with tips on top, she was raking in a lot of cash. The tips were good too; when people saved money on their meal, they were happy to give more to the staff, especially when they were good staff, such as Bethany.

The cash was mounting up, the flat of her own was getting closer, and somehow, amongst the music and shouting, Bethany finally fell asleep.

CHAPTER THREE

Two hundred miles away in Nottinghamshire, Stevie Johnson was also awake, and he knew why too. It was his twins, Henry and Aimee. Having just reached the age of two, they were both teething. It appeared that when one got it bad, the other got it worse. He loved them to bits, but the shrieking at three o'clock in the morning was stretching that love. Stevie looked across at Suzie, his wife. She was wearing an eye mask from a forgotten luxury exotic holiday some years ago, and she also had earplugs in.

Suzie hadn't even stirred. This was her style. As Stevie spent so much time away on the road, when he was at home it was his turn to sort out the kids. His look at Suzie wasn't one of love. Not just because of this moment, but because their marriage was failing. They had tried to pretend that the idea of having children would bring them together, but it hadn't worked.

Stevie jumped out of bed and went to the nursery – a perfect nursery that looked like it came straight from a magazine. Everything was the best quality and not a thing out of place, just like everything else his wife had organised in the house.

How he hated her.

He grabbed the bottle of liquid paracetamol on the side and measured out two doses. Aimee was crying the most, so he picked her up, gave her the medicine and put the dummy in her mouth. He followed the same procedure with Henry, their cries turning into whimpers almost straight away. Stevie wondered what exactly was in this magic liquid. He hadn't even heard of it two years ago, and now it was the most important item on their shopping list, and it knocked the kids out every time. Maybe it was better if he didn't think about what it contained. Holding one twin in the crook of each arm, he softly rocked them, wondering how long he would be able to hold them like this, as they were growing so fast.

His thoughts wandered to how much sleep he would get now. He had a long drive down to the south coast today, which was tiring enough without this interruption. Most wives would have been thoughtful and let him have a full night's sleep, but not Suzie.

How he hated her.

He was also starting to hate the life he had. If it weren't for the twins, he wasn't sure what he would have been doing by now.

It hadn't always been like this. Stevie had been outgoing and full of fun. At school, he'd been in every sports team and every musical production going, and he'd been popular with teachers, pupils and parents. He'd been so confident; there'd been no doubt he was going to be successful in later life.

His blond hair and blue eyes had also made him popular with the girls and then later on with the ladies. He never had a problem finding a partner; the only problem he had was getting rid of them in time for his next conquest, although sometimes those timings hadn't worked out properly. The fact that he had caused upset didn't really bother him.

Growing up in Mansfield around the time the coal industry was being shut down and all the pits were closing hadn't been ideal. He had loved going along to the miners' social clubs when he was little, and he had performed in quite a few of them in talent shows. But the heart of the community was being ripped out, and Stevie had known he didn't want to stay there long and that he would have to leave the area to seek any fame.

After leaving school, he had just started at drama college when a friend told him he was going to Butlin's to audition for a summer season at Skegness. Stevie went along, blew the judges away and got the job.

His pal didn't get a place, but it didn't bother Stevie.

He started the following week: six weeks' training, and then out on the ground, organising kids' clubs, running competitions, singing, dancing and generally being a bit of a star in the Butlin's world.

Everyone loved him – nans and granddads, all the way down to the kids, and in between were the teenage daughters and young mums. He had a choice of many and took up their offers, a different woman every night. Each one taking a little place in his heart until the next night. Stevie was having the time of his life and getting paid for it too.

After spending three years there, he decided to branch out in the world and travelled to Ibiza on a whim. He got a job at one of the massive clubs on the island. He started by dancing and performing and then worked out who were the most successful people there, got in with them and moved on to working the decks as a DJ. It was the beginning of another successful time in his life.

Ibiza was a party island, and Stevie loved to party. This

party lasted five years. When he decided to move back to the UK, he had lots of contacts in the business.

It was through this network that he became manager at Rockafellas nightclub in Sheffield, where he stayed for a few years, watching how the business developed, knowing exactly what he wanted to do next: own his own nightclub.

Together with some business associates, he bought Rockafellas and started to run it how he wanted. This was when he met Suzie. Tall, leggy and blonde, she turned up to do some promotional work. Stevie fell for her straight away, and the feeling was mutual. She was a model and had appeared topless a couple of times when she was younger. She was never forthcoming about what other photographic or film work she had partaken in, and Stevie never asked. It didn't matter; he was smitten.

He bought a luxury penthouse flat for them both to live in and was happy to fund her expensive needs when it came to clothes and beauty treatments and products. He'd thought that she was the one, and she thought so too. At least that's what she told him.

It was around that time that things started to go wrong. First, there were rumours that drug dealing was prevalent at the club. Stevie was the only partner who took a working interest, the others being happy to put up their money and gather the profits. So, he spoke to the local police and started a partnership to crack down on drug taking. It upset a lot of people, but it worked.

Nothing, however, would prepare him for the second problem. It was a normal Friday, around midnight, when a group of lads on a stag weekend turned up. They'd been out on the lash since lunchtime and were a bit boisterous, but the stag himself could hardly walk and was being dragged along by two of his pals. On seeing this and knowing that the area was covered by the police CCTV, the door staff refused to let them in. What happened next was all captured on those cameras, as well as the club's CCTV. Two of the group decided to have a go at the doormen, but not just verbally. They crossed the street to some nearby building works and helped themselves to a couple of three-foot scaffold poles.

The girls waiting in the queue screamed as the first man swung at the doormen and missed. Luckily, his aim was bad because of the amount of alcohol he'd consumed. The second man, Darren Andrews, decided drunkenly not to try to swing like his mate but instead to charge at the nearest doorman with the pole.

Yuri Gosmanov – six feet five, shaven headed and built like a brick outhouse – could look menacing, but the regulars all knew him as a gentle giant. He'd moved here from Latvia five years before, had got his SIA licence and worked the doors in Sheffield for the past three years.

Yuri had spotted Andrews and was ready for him. He grabbed the pole, and in one movement lifted it and spun his assailant round. It was so quick that Andrews lost his grip and flew off, landing flat on his back. The remnants of the queue cheered and laughed, no one noticing that as he landed in a crumpled heap on the ground, the back of his head hit the edge of the kerb.

Darren Andrews didn't move; in fact, he never moved again. The back of the skull is very soft and his had cracked like the shell of an egg, causing a brain bleed. He was rushed to Sheffield hospital, put on a life-support machine, but never regained consciousness. The machine was turned off three days later, and his organs were donated to save three other lives.

Yuri Gosmanov was arrested for murder. The charge was later changed to manslaughter, but Rockafellas was known as the 'Murder Nightclub' from then on.

It took the forensic teams a week to complete the scene, and then Stevie closed the nightclub for a few weeks to allow time for the funeral.

When it reopened, not only did hardly anyone turn up, but the victim's friends and family bombarded the local press and social media to try to get it closed. Although it stayed open, it lost money every day.

A month later, Stevie had a call at five o'clock in the morning from the police saying the club was on fire. By the time he got there, he could hardly recognise what was left of the building. When the fire brigade had finished putting the fire out, it was just rubble.

Fire investigators and crime-scene investigators deemed it suspicious. The fire had been started in two places and they also found traces of petrol, used as an accelerant, when they got to the bottom of the debris.

Stevie had honestly known nothing about the fire and had been able to provide an alibi when he was questioned by the police. He never found out who had ordered the arson, but it could have been one of the silent investors, worried about losing their money as the club went downhill.

The joke was that after all the debts had been sorted out, none of them had got much money back anyway, and all had got a lot less than they put in.

This meant that Stevie had ended up without a business, and was also unlikely to be able to get backing for any future ventures, as he was seen as a failure in the business world by those who had the money.

And none of it was his fault.

At least he had Suzie.

CHAPTER FOUR

The drive to Hastings didn't take long at night; indeed, it was only seventeen miles. During the day it could sometimes take an hour because of the sheer weight of traffic in this busy area, but at this time no such problems.

The journey took Crofts along the Marsh Road, and he could see out to sea as he drove past Pevensey Bay and Normans Bay, villages steeped in the history of smuggling.

As usual, the thought ran through his mind that with such a vast coastline it was impossible to monitor it in all places and modern-day smugglers were probably as busy as their predecessors, albeit with different cargoes. He had dealt with many large drugs jobs over the years in this area, but he guessed that many more illicit shipments were never found.

He drove through Little Common, a small village – just a roundabout and a few shops and houses. The road off to the left led to a football pitch where Oscar and his football team quite often played. The thought of it brought a smile to his face as he remembered watching the under-eleven leagues on a Sunday morning. The smile changed to a grin when he realised he had just thought of a place that had nothing to do with work.

Deborah always said he only knew his way around Sussex due to crime scenes. Crofts had noticed it too. Anywhere he went throughout the county, he could recollect working at a scene there, whether it was murder, robbery or burglary. He could never decide whether that was a good thing or not.

Before he knew it, he was through Bexhill and approaching the outskirts of Hastings. This took him on the road directly parallel with the sea. Crofts looked right and saw the reflection of the moonlight. It was dead calm like a millpond. In the distance there were a few lights, of ships passing through the English Channel. Crofts thought back to his time at sea during his previous career in the Royal Marines. He wondered where those ships were heading and how long they had been at sea.

Although there was satnav in the car, Crofts hadn't bothered to use it for this journey; he knew where he was going, having been to this area many times. As he approached the burnt-out pier, he took a left up the hill and into a mass of houses.

They were originally large town houses and must have been grand in their day, but most had been converted to flats over the years. These were now inhabited by a complete cross section of modern society. Some were still conventional family homes, but many had been bought up over the years by absentee landlords and just rented out to anyone.

When the rules governing social security payments were changed in the late eighties, it meant those on the dole could collect their payments wherever they liked rather than at their local office. The idea originally had been to get people on the road looking for work. What happened was that thousands of unemployed people moved from the larger cities to seaside resorts, allegedly looking for work but creating what became known as 'bail hostels'. It wasn't only on the south coast; it was the same all around the country. The landlords would buy the property and cram as many tenants in as possible, safe in the knowledge that all the rent would be paid by the government straight into their bank accounts.

It meant that the places weren't looked after properly and fell into disrepair. Many became dens of iniquity and hotbeds for criminals. The inhabitants had changed again over the last fifteen years as more and more foreigners had ended up in these places, bringing their own unique types of crime with them.

Crofts turned into the street he needed and looked for a patrol car, always a good direction indicator. He spotted one about a hundred metres further along and parked in front of it.

The police officer who was guarding the scene glanced over to see who was approaching at this time of the morning but then spotted the 'Scientific Support' decals on the side of the car. It meant he would have someone to chat to for a few minutes to break up the boredom of standing outside on his own.

Crofts jumped out of the car and bounded over to the scene guard. He was a dark-haired officer in his late thirties who Crofts had seen around the station in the past.

'Hi, mate. Have you been into the scene?' Crofts asked.

'No, it was the late shift who found the body, but they gave me an update for you.'

'Fire away then,' said Crofts.

'We received a call from a call box along the street around 2230 hours. All they said was "Jonny is dead at the squat". When asked which squat, this address was quoted. The control-room assistant asked them to stay on the line, but they put the phone down straight away.'

He paused and looked up and down the street before continuing. 'It was a busy time of night and no units were free, so it was half an hour before anyone attended. On arrival, they realised something was up. The same unit had attended that same address several times in the past fortnight, and there were always loads of people around. But last night there was nobody. They waited for another unit to arrive, then entered the building using torches. It's a dangerous place in the dark; floorboards missing, discarded needles all over the place – a complete health hazard – but as it had been called in as a death, they decided they needed to have a look.'

He listened to a broadcast from his radio, before continuing again. 'The place was empty, but on the second floor there was the body. The officers know him. He's a Lithuanian called Jonny, although his real name is Jonas Petrauskas. Entered the country three years ago on a work permit, then miraculously disappeared, to be later found living the high life in a squat in Hastings.'

The PC laughed at his own joke, and Crofts smiled too. He knew enough about these types of people, having spent the last few years dealing with their problems.

'Anyway, to continue,' he said, reverting back to his reporting officer mode, as most PCs did when reciting accounts, 'the victim was lying on the floor with a syringe sticking out of his arm. They checked for a pulse, and there wasn't one. Paramedics had arrived just before and tried to resuscitate and also tried a defibrillator, but to no avail. One of the paramedics confirmed death at 2312 precisely. You'll be glad to know that everyone then left the building, leaving everything in situ, and they started the scene log.'

'Thank God for that,' Crofts replied. 'At least all of my forensic training is finally sinking in.'

In the past there had been problems with scene preservation. Police officers had a habit of 'just taking a look', which meant items were moved, sometimes completely ruining the continuity of scenes. Over the years, Crofts had lectured on most of the training courses the police ran, instructing student officers right through to detective sergeants, and it was good to see that most of what he had taught was finally being put into practice.

'How bad is the access once in the scene?' Crofts asked.

'Very hazardous. I went in last week and was only on the ground floor, and that was bad enough.'

The conversation was halted by the sound of an engine racing up the hill towards them. It was Hannah Jukes arriving in a Ford Connect van, silver grey with 'Scientific Support' signage emblazoned all over. She wasn't speeding at all; it was just that it was the only vehicle moving at that time of morning, so it sounded louder than normal.

Hannah pulled up alongside Crofts' car and walked over to the two of them. She was small, only just over five feet tall, brown hair and eyes. Before joining the department, she had worked as an air stewardess.

'Thanks for getting here so quickly,' Crofts called, and then added with a grin, 'nice to see you have made yourself as glamorous as possible.'

Hannah poked her tongue out at him in jest. As with all of the girls in the department, she didn't wear make-up and her hair was pulled back into a ponytail.

'How much do you know about this job?' Crofts asked.

'Only what the irritatingly happy controller told me on the phone, and then I came straight here,' Hannah said.

'Yes, I had the same, but anyway, there's some good news and bad news. The bad news is the place is a shithole and it's going to take us a while to even get to the body, so we're up for the rest of the day.'

'Fantastic. The overtime will go towards my holiday in Thailand!'

'The good news is that we won't be entering the building until daylight, so we've got plenty of time to get sorted.'

'Great,' said Hannah. 'I'll go and start taking some

photographs of the outside of the building, then we'll be ready to go inside when we have more light.'

'Sounds good to me,' said Crofts, glad Hannah was one of the staff who could take the initiative and didn't need to have every single action spelled out to her.

Crofts walked back to his car and started making notes on what he had learnt so far. He contacted the control room to let them know he and Hannah would be at the scene for some time.

He then put on his PPE – personal protective equipment; the white 'bunny suit', as the SOCOs called them – together with overshoes, gloves, a mask and hairnet. This protection was to stop him from contaminating the scene by leaving his DNA or fingerprints, but at jobs like this one, and many others, it was also a barrier against picking up anything unpleasant in the scene.

It was, he mused, one of those places that you wiped your feet on the way out rather than on the way in.

CHAPTER FIVE

Bethany was woken by the sound of her alarm clock. She'd had about five hours' sleep, but it didn't feel like it. She had to get up early in the mornings, firstly to get her make-up on, which took long enough, but secondly to walk to the town centre to catch the bus to Pevensey Bay.

That was the only problem with this job: the location. Bethany had to rely on public transport most of the time. In some ways it wasn't too bad, as she could choose bus or train; it was just that she was ruled by the timetables. If she missed a bus, it was an hour wait for the next. She wished she could afford a car. Several of the others working at The Moorings had recently passed their driving tests and were lucky enough to have parents who helped them buy one. Yet another reason for her to wish she had grown up as part of a normal family.

Maybe it was something else she could eventually afford if she worked hard enough. It was up to her.

The reason she was happy to suffer the awkwardness of public transport was that she loved working there. Bethany could have found a job in a shop in the town centre to save her that hassle, but she wouldn't have been able to work the hours she currently did. Malcolm and Sandy were good employers and were happy to let their staff work as long as possible. They needed good, reliable people, and Bethany was one of them.

On top of that, it was well paid, and with the extra bonus of tips. Bethany had never been scared of hard work, and with all the cash she was earning, her dream of that flat of her own, and even a car, was getting nearer.

It was just after eight, and the rest of the Foyer was quiet, last night's fun and frolics still being slept off throughout the building.

Bethany felt like putting her music on loud just to get them back for the noise she had to put up with in the early hours, but she wasn't like that, and anyway, if someone came to complain to her, she still didn't have any make-up on, and she couldn't have that.

She took a sip from her can of energy drink and opened a packet of cheese and onion crisps. This was breakfast Bethany-style. It was all she wanted at that time of day. Some of her foster families had made wonderful breakfasts, but as she had also spent a lot of time in children's homes, the sight of a cooked breakfast with congealed fat because it had been left on a hot plate for several hours had put her off anything like that for life.

They were given meals at The Moorings anyway, so this would keep her going until then. Yet another perk. She decided that one day, when she had made enough money to rent a flat and get a car, she would like to run a pub, and if she did, she would run it just like Malcolm and Sandy did.

Bethany showered and now started on the make-up, transforming herself from an odd-looking person to an exotic-looking young woman.

She was self-taught. Not for her the instructions of the snooty cows on the make-up stands in Debenhams, who wouldn't have spoken to her anyway. They always managed to look down their noses long enough to decide she wasn't someone who would be buying much. The joke was that Bethany used a lot of products, so they actually missed out on a large number of sales from her. She just went over to the cheaper stores and got value for money.

The process used to take her about an hour, but she had started to cut this down a little and so was ready to go at about nine o'clock. This gave her half an hour to walk to the bus stop, which was plenty of time. She put on the black leggings and black T-shirt that were her uniform, locked her room and made her way down to the main entrance.

'Here she is!' said Ronnie, the duty manager, talking to a staff member Bethany had not seen before, who turned around to look.

The attention made Bethany blush. She wasn't sure whether it was the fact that they were both looking at her, or the fact that Ronnie liked to flirt with her. She could feel her reddening cheeks and just hoped her barrier layer of make-up hid them. Unfortunately, her make-up did not cover her neck, which had gone crimson. Ronnie enjoyed the fact that he could embarrass her so easily, but he actually did like Bethany a lot.

'This is Josie, just starting here today,' Ronnie said. 'I was telling her that you would be the first resident to show your face this morning.'

Josie smiled and said hello. She was in her fifties, with badly dyed blonde hair and a face that showed she had led a hard life. Bethany liked the look of her but didn't show it. Years of meeting new people in different situations had taught her to be wary until she had got to know them.

'Bethany is off to work, unlike a lot of the little darlings who live here,' said Ronnie.

'Where is it you work?' asked Josie, with what appeared to be genuine interest.

'The Moorings at Pevensey Bay,' replied Bethany, still a little cautious but already warming to her.

'The pub on the beach,' sang Josie in the style of the jingle that was constantly played on the local Sovereign FM station. 'I love it there. Nothing better on a summer's evening than sitting outside on the beach with a nice glass of wine. The meals are so cheap too.'

'I know,' chipped in Ronnie. 'I still can't work out how they make a profit.'

'Sorry,' said Bethany. 'Must go or I'll miss the bus.'

'Of course,' he replied. 'What time are you working till tonight?'

'Ten o'clock.'

'Wow,' said Josie. 'That's a long shift. I didn't think you were allowed to work that long nowadays.'

Ronnie answered for Bethany, as it was obvious that she was itching to go. 'No, you're not, but who cares if you're getting paid, hey, Bethany?'

'Yes,' she replied, heading out the door and into the morning air, glad to get away from a conversation that might end up with her being asked what she was going to do with all that money. No one knew about her plans, and Ronnie was the last person to tell, as he was a terrible gossip.

It was her secret, but it was getting closer by the day.

CHAPTER SIX

S tevie was also up and about early for the long drive down to the south coast. The interruption to his sleep hadn't really affected him, since the twins had dropped off almost straight away thanks to the Calpol.

Stevie had a spring in his step because he would be getting away from Suzie for a few days. As much as he loved the little ones, he couldn't stand the atmosphere between the two of them. He wasn't sure why it had all turned sour, but he had the feeling that his drop in status from nightclub owner to medical rep had something to do with it.

The financial side of his life had completely gone up in smoke along with his beloved club. The smart apartment had had to be sold, and they had ended up renting.

Although this was a high-end apartment and up to Suzie's expectations, in Stevie's mind it was costing far too much and was another not needed extravagance. She still wanted all the trappings they had been used to; he just didn't have any money coming in.

The problem was that his former status as a top DJ and nightclub owner wasn't any use to him when he went to job interviews. His was a 'who you know' type of world, and no one wanted to know Stevie after the disaster of Rockafellas.

People who suddenly found themselves out of work would usually be happy to take any menial job as long as it brought in some cash, but Stevie couldn't. In her materialistic life, Suzie would never be able to cope with anything she saw as inferior. This led to the first few arguments.

She couldn't cope with the fact that the successful Stevie she had first met wouldn't always be able to lead that lifestyle, and when he started to tell her about some of the jobs he was applying for, she couldn't deal with it. The main thing was that money was required, and she wanted more, so Stevie started looking outside of his previous career for something he could build on in the future.

As always with Stevie, he had another stroke of luck. There wasn't much happening on the job front, so he decided to take Suzie out for lunch to cheer them up. He still knew lots of people in Sheffield and could get a table at VeroGusto, a smart Italian restaurant on Norfolk Row. Suzie ordered champagne, and Stevie had a brand-new credit card in his pocket.

He was barely into his first drink when he became aware of someone staring at him from across the room. He looked familiar, but Stevie couldn't place him. The gent saw his look and strolled over, hand outstretched ready to shake.

'Stevie, my old mate. I haven't seen you since school!' the stranger boomed.

Stevie remained unsure who he was.

'How's things with you? The last time I heard you were running Rockafellas.'

'That's all over,' Stevie managed to get in before his new friend continued, 'Do you fancy sharing lunch with me and Naomi?'

Stevie looked over and saw a blonde woman, maybe twenty

years old, almost a younger version of Suzie, sitting looking embarrassed on her own.

He glanced at Suzie, but she was already on her second glass of fizz so would agree to anything.

'Okay, mate, we'll move over,' he replied, still trying to remember the guy's name.

Fortunately, the day was saved when the man introduced himself to Suzie, kissing her on the hand in a way that many women wouldn't have enjoyed, but after a couple of glasses on an empty stomach, she responded to happily.

'I'm Freddie Ashworth,' he said. 'Used to go to school with Stevie. We had some great times, didn't we, mate?'

'We certainly did!' said Stevie with relief, although he was unable to think of what great times he and Freddie had shared.

Naomi appeared glad of the company. Wearing immaculate make-up, smartly dressed, but obviously bored with Freddie's company, she looked at Suzie like she was the answer to her prayers. They ordered another bottle of champagne, along with some starters, and then Freddie began to tell Stevie what had happened to him since they last met. There was no chance Stevie was going to get a word in edgeways.

Freddie had left school with no qualifications and had got a job in a local care home. He'd spent the first year or so doing everything needed. Whether it was washing up in the kitchens or washing old people's bottoms in their rooms. He was a cheery lad, and the old folks loved him. Freddie also loved them, and he couldn't believe he had a job he enjoyed so much. He'd even moved into a small room at the back of the home near the kitchens, as it was better than living at home.

Within a year or two, Freddie had become the manager. As he knew the business inside out, the owner of the company had been glad to have someone he could rely on. He'd paid for

Freddie to go to college to get himself a business diploma and then helped him understand the financial side of things.

When the owner died, he left Freddie a fair amount of cash, which Freddie had used to buy a care home of his own. His attention to detail meant everyone who stayed there had a great life, and word spread. Freddie had bought two more homes in that first year and started Ashworth Healthcare, which had been very successful.

He now had ten homes and a thriving business. He also invested in a property portfolio, which, as with everything with Freddie, was also successful.

Stevie zoned out of Freddie's story to check on what Suzie and Naomi were talking about. All he heard was the word 'shoes' and he knew the two of them obviously had a connection that would keep them occupied for a while.

Finally, during the main course, Freddie stopped talking about himself to tuck into the delicious-looking fillet steak that he had ordered, and managed to say, 'So, what you up to now, Stevie?'

Stevie gave him an abridged version on his life so far, making it sound successful, exotic and exciting. It appeared that Freddie loved every minute of it.

Stevie managed to turn Rockafellas' final demise into such a tragedy that he was sure he saw a tear in Freddie's eye.

'What you going to do now?' asked Freddie.

'I honestly don't know,' Stevie replied sadly. 'I'm obviously not going to get back into that type of business around here. I just want a normal job for a change. Believe it or not, I've never really had one. I'd like to settle down, get a nice place and live quietly for once.'

Freddie appeared to be deep in thought. Stevie suspected he had many contacts, although these were likely to be in the healthcare business, which wasn't really what Stevie was interested in. But then Freddie suddenly smiled and asked earnestly, 'What do you know about drugs?'

'I just told you: that was the reason everything started to go wrong.'

'No, sorry, not those types of drugs. I mean pharmaceuticals.'

'What about them?' Stevie asked, interest filtering through the boozy haze.

'I was talking to a mate of mine the other day. He was bemoaning the fact that he can never get decent pharmaceutical sales reps, and yet it's a gold mine. Those big drug companies have so much money sloshing about but can never get the right people. You would be good at it. You've always had the gift of the gab, and once you know the subject, you'd be ideal.'

'Not something I would have thought of,' Stevie admitted. He had rather hoped Freddie would have had something in his own line of business.

'No, me neither, but the more I think of it, the more it suits you. Those companies need people like you. There's so much money to be earned. Don't forget, you'll be basically your own boss, and there will be a company car. I've heard some of the bonuses that are paid when a big deal is done are large and will pay for nice holidays. What I've learnt in business, and life in general, is that I make snap decisions, and most of them turn out good, and anyway, it'll start you up again, even if you don't like it. You can move on once you've got yourself established. Now I think of it, it's a no-brainer!'

Freddie stopped and stared at Stevie. He looked happy that he had found a solution for his 'old friend'.

Stevie thought about it and warmed to the idea but then realised there may be a problem. 'The only thing is, those sorts of jobs are mainly commission based, and at the moment I have to pay a lot of money for our apartment.'

'No problem,' said Freddie. 'I've quite a few properties I own and rent out. I could lease you one at a cheap rate until you get established.'

'That's a great proposal,' said Stevie, but, glancing at Suzie, he added, 'Unfortunately we have to look for something high quality.'

Freddie noticed the glance and for the first time looked at Suzie and listened to what Stevie was saying. That sort of thing wouldn't stop him, though. He'd dealt with plenty of women like her over the years.

'Suzie, love, can I just ask you a quick question?'

'Of course you can,' she replied. She appeared to be liking the attention and was already warming to this successful businessman.

'Have you ever thought of living out in the country, in a little village?'

'Do you know,' she replied, trying not to slur, 'that was always a dream of mine since I was a little girl.'

Stevie couldn't decide what to make of that; it was the first time he had ever heard her mention it.

'Well,' continued Freddie, 'I might be able to make your dream come true. I've just completed a barn conversion on the outskirts of Church Warsop. It's all top spec, just waiting for someone to rent it out to.'

'Sounds lovely.'

'Even better, we're only a few miles away, so you and Naomi can meet up and go shopping together.'

Suzie's day had just turned into the best she'd had for a long time. She wasn't interested in whatever kind of job Stevie was getting. She was already planning what she would need to buy for the barn conversion. It was definitely a yes from her.

At the end of the lunch, to complete the perfect day,

Freddie had paid the substantial bill and wouldn't take a penny towards it. He had just been glad to help his old friend.

Things moved fast with Freddie. Within a week Stevie had had an interview with Pfizer and got the job, and within a fortnight they had moved into Moses Farm, the property Freddie had promised them.

Life would be rosy again.

CHAPTER SEVEN

In Hastings, Hannah and Crofts had been busy. While he continued to update his notes and started to compose a forensic strategy, Hannah had photographed the whole of the outside area and was ready to go inside.

The strategy was something that would dictate how the scene would be dealt with: what photographs were needed, what type of examinations they would undertake, and what exhibits they would need to recover. Crofts would later agree it with the SIO, who would then use it as part of his crime policy.

It was important that all actions were recorded properly in case there were any problems or queries later in the enquiry. Although Crofts had not actually been in the building or seen the body at this stage, he knew enough facts to get plenty of the outline down. He knew from experience that it was best to record as much as possible during any downtime in an enquiry; when things got busier later, he would struggle to find time to make notes.

Hannah came over and showed him the photographs she had taken so far on the camera's display. Crofts was impressed with the images. When he'd started as a SOCO, not that long ago, it was before the advent of digital cameras, and he'd had to use wet film. In a situation such as this, with little light, you would need to use all your photography know-how to get your pictures to come out correctly. You would then have to wait before they were processed and sent to you. It could take weeks, although on serious jobs they were able to get them developed the same day. Nowadays you could look at images in situ and make sure everything was correct.

Back in those days, one poor SOCO managed to photograph a murder scene without putting film in his camera. There were definite disciplinary procedures on that one.

As it was now getting brighter by the minute, Crofts told Hannah to get the large lamp ready and headed towards the building.

'Who you gonna call?' said the PC on the front door as they approached.

At first Crofts didn't click, but then he realised that he and Hannah were fully suited, masked and gloved, carrying lamps, torches and a camera and did actually look like they were from the movie.

'SOCObusters!' replied Crofts.

The scene guard gave a loud laugh that echoed around the quiet, empty street. He was holding the scene log and added the names Crofts and Jukes to the list.

Crofts quickly checked the log to see who had been in the scene. Even though it was normally started in a rush at the beginning of a scene, the log was very important. In the past, scene logs had been introduced in court by clever barristers trying to intimate that someone had or hadn't been into a scene, depending on their defence.

Crofts hated barristers with a vengeance. He could never understand how they slept at night after defending clients he knew were guilty, but that was how the legal system worked.

There was no way he was going to give a lawyer an easy way into his evidence by making a mistake in something as simple as the scene log.

Once past the scene guard, he switched on the heavy torch, which lit up the hallway. As far as the eye could see there was rubbish. There were empty bottles everywhere. No need to look at the labels; they would all be the same few brands of strong, cheap cider.

A few years before there had been a period where every murder scene over a couple of months had had a bottle of cheap white cider. It got to be an in-joke amongst the SOCOs. One day they attended the scene of an alcoholic's suspicious death, and no one could believe it – there weren't any bottles in his flat. It seemed unreal. Just before they left, someone checked the dustbin outside. It contained three bin liners full of empty white cider bottles. It turned out that the poor man's mother had found him dead in bed and had tidied up before calling the police as she didn't want them seeing her son's habit.

No one had tidied up in this building, though. In amongst the empty bottles were carrier bags, rotting food and yes, even human faeces.

'Lovely,' Crofts heard Hannah say behind him.

'What did you expect?' said Crofts. 'Some luxury apartment? It is Hastings remember!'

Hannah laughed and began to take photos as Crofts pointed the large lamp in different directions. The idea was to try to capture the scene in as much detail as possible. SOCOs were taught to quarter the room, which meant to take a photo from each corner and then focus in on any relevant items. Whether it was a burglary or a murder scene, the procedures were the same.

Crofts could see stains on several walls. Those may have to be checked a little closer later, depending on what was decided in the forensic strategy. If this was in a normal domestic home, they could prove important, but in this type of place, probably not.

There would probably have been plenty of disputes, assaults and beatings in the last few months, which would have led to blood and other bodily fluids being left on the walls, skirting boards and doors of the building, none of which would have been cleaned up, and none of which would help them in this case.

As always in these types of scenes, there was plenty of what the police recorded as 'drugs paraphernalia' in their reports. That meant used needles, burnt pieces of kitchen foil, burnt spoons and many other items used by addicts. This was yet another reason to be careful. Crofts reminded Hannah, knowing that sometimes SOCOs were so intent on capturing the correct images that they forgot simple safety precautions.

Crofts headed for the stairs. The reports had told them that the body was on an upper floor, so they were photographing their way towards it. At this stage there was no interest in what was in the other rooms on the floor, but later in the day all rooms would need photographing and searching. Now, the body waiting for them on the first floor was the most important part of the scene.

At the foot of the stairs, Crofts could see that many of the floorboards were missing in the steps. These would have been used to make fires to keep warm and to cook drugs. He told Hannah to stop taking photographs for a while so he could use the torch to see where he was going as they both gingerly climbed the stairs.

They arrived at the first-floor landing, and without looking any further, it was obvious that the rooms would be in a similar state to those on the ground floor. They continued to both video and photograph their way up to the next floor. Crofts could see rooms in all directions. He decided to start on the left and work his way clockwise around.

'We'll number these rooms from one to six, starting with this one,' he said, half telling himself and half telling Hannah.

He tensed a little, knowing he was approaching a dead body. Crofts had dealt with hundreds of them over the years, but this moment, just before he actually saw the body, was always a little unreal, as you never knew what you were about to find.

Despite this, Crofts had always believed SOCOs were lucky compared with the police officers, who would often find a body when not prepared for it.

The first two rooms were the same as all the others, but Crofts could see a pair of dirty trainers and jeans on the floor as he walked through the third doorway. There were also flies buzzing around the room. He stopped and signalled to Hannah that this was the one so that she could prepare herself as well.

Continuing to video, while Hannah photographed from the doorway, Crofts approached the body and took some close-ups. They then stopped for a second and had a look at the victim. He was probably in his early thirties, wearing grubby clothes, and weighing a couple of stones too few. Nothing untoward there. He looked the same as most of the addicts Crofts had seen, but there were two things that rang alarm bells. Firstly, the victim had quite a lot of bruising to the face, a black eye and a cut across the nose, which looked fresh. Secondly, he had a syringe stuck in his left arm. These two details meant that this would have to be treated as suspicious.

The injuries indicated a possible assault, and they would also have to establish who injected the syringe, as it was possible that someone had killed the victim with an overdose.

As Crofts shone his torch around the face, he could see bluebottles had laid their eggs in the eye wound and maggots were already hatching to start devouring the body. Those flies would have landed within seconds of the victim's last breath and would continue to do so. The conditions of the room meant that there were plenty there already, so they would soon multiply.

Hannah took more close-ups of the body, whilst Crofts continued examining it. There was no need for him to tell her what to do. He trusted all of his staff to know what was needed in these situations.

He took a couple of steps back and out of the room to use his mobile phone, scrolling through his contacts until he found Tom Mead's number. It was answered on the first ring. The SIO was waiting for this call.

'Hi, guv, it's Simon Crofts. Just giving you an update.'

'What have you got there, mate?'

'Guv, we're going to have to call it as sus. The victim's got bruising on his face, and there is a needle stuck into his arm. The Crown Prosecution Service stated a few months ago that they want all these types of drugs deaths to be investigated fully from the off.'

In the past, too many cases had been written off too early just because drugs were involved, meaning that sometimes serious crimes had been missed.

'That's okay,' Mead said. 'I'll set the wheels in motion at this end. Anything you need from me?'

'No, I'm fine. I'll let the coroner know and arrange a Home Office post-mortem. I'll let you know the details when I get them.'

'Okay, thanks for that. Once I've arranged a few things this end, I'll come over and meet you at the scene.'

'No problem,' Crofts said, and then finished the call. He knew there was a lot to do but that there would be a large amount of hanging around. He was also hungry, as it was now eight o'clock.

'If you've got to a stage where you can stop, then do, and we'll go for some brekkie,' he called out to Hannah.

'I'm on my way,' she replied.

Crofts went outside, took off his bunny suit, mask and overshoes, and headed to his car. He had a couple of phone calls to make before eating.

CHAPTER EIGHT

After a half-hour walk, Bethany was on the bus. She liked the fact that it was the terminus, so she was one of the first on and able to choose her seat.

Bethany always went straight to the corner back seat, hoping no one would want to sit next to her. There were only a couple of others on the bus, and it seemed as though they all wanted to sit alone.

As the journey started, and the bus pulled in at each stop, Bethany watched people getting on, ready to give them a look if they came towards her. As usual no one did. The sight of her, early morning, in full make-up, giving that look was enough to scare most people off. Indeed, the only ones who ever came near her were the nutters, but luckily, none were around today.

The journey continued, and as the bus approached Pevensey Bay, Bethany felt warm inside, as she did every time she arrived. It was a lovely old-fashioned seaside place, and it provided her with a job, money, security and what could loosely be called 'friends'.

Bethany got off at the bus stop in the centre of the village and walked across to the small side street where The Moorings was located.

As the advert implied, the pub was literally on the beach. The large conservatory that had been added across the front of the building, now reflecting the early morning sun, made the place look even brighter. The view directly out to the English Channel was amazing whatever the time of day or, indeed, year.

Bethany went in through the staff entrance at the back, meaning she would have to walk through the kitchen. This sometimes caused her problems, as some of the kitchen staff teased her. Today, all was okay; only the owner Malcolm and Eddy, one of the boss's young protégés, were there.

'All right, treacle?' Eddy called. He was seventeen, dark haired and stocky. It was how he welcomed most of the waitresses, and he always had a grin on his face.

Bethany smiled, said a quick yes and hurried through to the main bar area, where Sandy was already busy setting up tables for the lunches, as diners would be arriving shortly.

Malcolm and Sandy had taken over The Moorings five years ago, when it had been dying on its feet after the previous owners had let it go downhill. In the past, it had been a family-friendly pub that had attracted holidaymakers from the campsites nearby and, more importantly, local families out of season.

Malcolm and Sandy had taken over several similar businesses in the past few years and made them all a success. Their technique was to change an ailing pub into a restaurant. Get rid of any problem drinkers, then put on a simple menu of good food and charge silly prices. Within weeks it had been full again.

It also appealed to the blue-rinse brigade – pensioners – of which the area had plenty: they knew a bargain. The Moorings also attracted the family crowd in the evenings, and for any celebrations.

Bethany loved it. She liked the owners, she liked the customers, and got on all right with most of the staff. There had been a few moments with one or two to start with, mainly down to her not wanting to join in with the group on nights out and the like, but once they had realised that it wasn't because she didn't like them but because she preferred her own company, everything was fine.

The owners loved her. She had good experience in the trade and was punctual and well-motivated, which couldn't be said for all the teenage staff. Bethany had helped them out so many times when others had let them down that Sandy, she knew, thought the world of her. Her unusual look didn't put Sandy off; Bethany was a good worker, and they were hard to come by.

Bethany got straight to work as soon as she had taken her jacket off, preparing the tables for the upcoming busy lunchtime.

Two other girls, who had been chatting about boyfriends (or lack of them), saw what Bethany was doing and stirred themselves to join in. This made Sandy smile. Bethany was one member of staff who was essential to the business.

CHAPTER NINE

The phone calls Crofts had to make were to change his diary for the day. This happened often.

His day-to-day role as a senior SOCO was to run a base in the east of the county with his fellow senior, Maria Milligan. They dealt with the tasking of the staff, as well as giving advice on anything required for the normal-volume crime or any serious crime that was happening at any moment throughout their area, creating forensic strategies when needed.

It also meant dealing with all the personnel problems that came with an office of twenty staff, of which there were many. They were very busy, but it all stopped when a major crime came in. This was when there was a change of hats, so to speak, and they became crime-scene managers.

As all thoughts were now on that major crime, everything else had to be put on the back-burner, but it was always still there. Sometimes a senior might pick up several major crimes in a row, so it was hard to keep up to speed with all that was going on.

Crofts often felt like a plate spinner at the circus. Ensuring all areas were covered was the most stressful part of his job, and there were times when it was hard to keep on top of it all, but it was also what made his job so good: there was always plenty to do.

All he needed to do this morning was cancel a CID inspectors' meeting, which wasn't too bad. Several of the others meant to be attending would also be cancelling due to the overnight job.

The other cancellation was the PDR of one of his staff, Leighton Phillips. The personal development review was dreamt up by someone at HQ some years before. It probably seemed like a good idea on paper and for supervisors and their staff in office roles, but it didn't work for those in operational roles.

It was too long-winded and didn't really record what was needed in their work. Crofts was a very conscientious supervisor and knew his staff were the most important part of his job and that their development was paramount. He knew how they all performed from working with them constantly; he didn't need to fill in the never-ending forms that were requested. The staff didn't like them either. It was, to most of them, a time-wasting procedure, only needed when going for promotion. Cynicism was something that the police were good at.

So, his call to Leighton was an easy one, especially as he also had to ask him to meet him and Hannah at the scene, as it was common practice to have a senior and two SOCOs at a major incident.

Crofts had a friendly dig at the big Welshman: 'That's if you're not too injured.'

Leighton, like most of his countrymen, loved his rugby, although he would quite often end up with some type of injury after playing. Bruises, cuts and sprains were a weekly occurrence, but having a boss who came from an ex-services background meant that he didn't get a lot of sympathy. In fact, Crofts was more likely to take the mickey. Leighton didn't mind, knowing it was just a bit of fun. He didn't mention the dead leg he'd received the day before and said he would get to the scene as soon as possible.

Crofts was happy. He knew with Hannah and Leighton he had a good team for the day. He would also have to call forensic pathology services to arrange a pathologist, but he knew it was a waste of time trying to contact them before nine o'clock. So, it was time for breakfast.

Hannah jumped in the car with him, and they drove to the nearest McDonald's. Crofts wasn't a fan of fast food, but when you had already been up a few hours, a Golden Arch breakfast hit the spot.

They bought their meals and sat down to eat, watching the comings and goings of the morning rush. Having been at a crime scene with a dead body only minutes ago, Crofts found it surreal that they were now surrounded by salesmen, hung-over builders, stressed mums and schoolchildren all munching away on their favourite breakfasts. They'd never guess what Crofts and Hannah had been dealing with that morning while they were still tucked up in their beds.

Before they left, they both used the toilets, something else learnt over the years. There were never toilet facilities at scenes, especially at houses like their current workplace, so the timing of toilet breaks was almost as important as eating and drinking. It was then time to head back to the scene.

As it was now after nine, Crofts called forensic pathology services. Although the company was based in Oxford, the forensic pathologists worked in different parts of the country. There were only ten forensic pathologists covering the whole of the south of England, all highly trained in criminal post-mortems and able to interpret injuries and, most importantly, establish the cause of death. Their daily work was to carry out general post-mortems at their local mortuary.

Whenever there was a major crime, and a Home Office forensic post-mortem was needed, one of these specialists would be called.

Unfortunately, because of their location and their large workload, there was always a long wait for them, which couldn't be helped. That was why Crofts wanted to phone early: he wanted to get the ball rolling.

He got through to Jean at FPS, who treated him like an old friend. Although they had never met, they spoke to each other most weeks, making it feel as if they had. Jean listened to what Crofts had to say about his scene and then agreed to get back to him once she had checked which pathologists were available.

This was the normal sequence of events, but Crofts was also aware that the death of a druggie in Hastings wasn't going to be high on the pathologists' list of job priorities, and if more important PMs were needed in other areas, his would be knocked further down the list.

The call back from Jean came within a couple of minutes, which was always a good sign. Doctor Andrew Eaton was available but would be travelling from Poole, in Dorset. Crofts tried not to sound too disappointed.

It wasn't so much the waiting time that he was unhappy with, as there was always a wait; it was the name. Doctor Eaton was one of the slowest, most thorough pathologists around. This meant that it was going to be an even longer day.

Jean asked Crofts if he could ring Doctor Eaton and whether he knew his number.

'Unfortunately, yes!' replied Crofts, which made Jean chuckle, as everyone knew what Eaton was like.

Andrew Eaton answered his mobile on the first ring. He obviously wasn't busy, as pathologists took ages to answer if they were involved in a post-mortem. Like Jean, the pathologist spoke to Crofts as if he were an old friend, although in his case they had met many times.

Eaton listened to Crofts' briefing on what had happened at the scene. 'That sounds fairly straightforward to me, although I will be travelling from Poole by train, so it'll be a while before I get to you.'

'Will you need to see the body in situ?' asked Crofts, already knowing the answer.

'No, that's okay. As long as you take plenty of photos, I can look at them at the mortuary.'

The pathologists that Crofts had encountered in his early years had always wanted to see the body in situ, but these days they didn't. It was partly because the earlier pathologists would get more involved in the whole case, whereas nowadays they were too busy and always needed to get on with other things. Actually, it helped Crofts, because it meant that he and his team could now get on with processing the scene whilst waiting for the arrival of Doctor Eaton.

'Hopefully I can catch the eleven o'clock train, which should mean I arrive at Hastings at around four thirty,' Doctor Eaton said. 'Will you be able to pick me up from the station?'

'Of course. I'll see you there, Doc,' replied Crofts, smiling to himself.

The cost of a Home Office PM was over two thousand pounds, and the pathologists were hardly low paid, but Dr Eaton would always ask for a lift to save the cost of a taxi fare.

CHAPTER TEN

Now that their break was over, Crofts and Hannah headed back to the scene, arriving at the same time as Leighton Phillips, the SIO, Tom Mead, and his deputy SIO, Alison Williams.

Leighton had already prepared a full set of PPE for them to wear. It always made Crofts chuckle watching CID officers struggling to get into bunny suits. For the SOCOs, it was their daily outfit, but for those not used to them they were a problem, especially for women like Alison who wore a skirt and heels.

Once everyone was fully rigged, they walked into the outer scene, signing the log on their way through. Out of public earshot, Crofts gave the SIOs an update on everything found so far and told them what had been done within the scene. The fact that it had been fully videoed and photographed meant that everyone was able to move around the scene easily.

When they arrived at the body, Tom had a good look and agreed with Crofts' synopsis.

'It has to be dealt with as a suspicious death at this time, until we can prove otherwise. I'm happy for you to continue along those lines,' he said.

Crofts told him about the arrangements for the post-mortem, adding it would be held at Hastings mortuary.

'Great, I'll see you there,' said Mead.

That pleased Crofts. Some of the newer SIOs sent their deputies to PMs. He couldn't understand how someone in charge of an enquiry would not attend one of the most important parts of it, but Tom Mead wasn't like that. He wanted to know everything that was going on. Some SOCOs might even say Mead went over the top, but Crofts didn't agree. In his eyes there could never be a thorough enough investigation.

'Oh, by the way, we now have an operational name. It's Op Dundee,' Alison told him.

Operational names were decided by the force control room. Apparently, a list was already compiled, a bit like for hurricanes. The names often sounded funny at first, but after a few days, with everyone on the enquiry using it, the name would fit the case. No one knew who compiled the list and how.

Whilst Hannah and Leighton helped the detectives out of their PPE, Crofts busied himself with several phone calls. Firstly, he contacted the coroner's officer, John Snow, in Hastings.

Coroners, whose role dated back to the twelfth century, were required to investigate all deaths before issuing the formal death certificate. Coroner's officers gathered most of that information for them, in preparation for the coroner's court. As their paths crossed quite often, Crofts and John knew each other well.

'Hello, Snowy, it's Simon,' said Crofts to the former police officer, whom he had known for most of his service. Although his nickname had originally come about because of his surname, the name fitted him even better now that his hair had turned white with age.

'I was waiting for you to call. I saw on the log that you had been to the scene,' said Snowy.

'Well, you know the background then. The SIO has agreed that we'll treat it as sus. I've arranged for Andrew Eaton to carry out the PM at the mortuary around five this afternoon.'

'I take it this is you asking for permission from the coroner to proceed,' said Snowy. It was a gentle jibe at Crofts, because technically he should have asked for the coroner's permission before making any of the arrangements so far. However, there was enough experience on both sides for them to trust each other.

'Of course,' said Crofts sarcastically. 'I would hate to have to do your job for you!'

He heard a chuckle at the other end of the phone. It was a conversation they had had many times before, and to be honest, Crofts knew that Snowy was happy to let him take a step ahead. Unlike some of the newer senior SOCOs, who wanted the coroner's officers to do everything for them.

'Can you do me a favour?' asked Crofts. 'Can you let them know in the mortuary and make sure it's okay?'

'No problem, mate,' replied Snowy. 'The morticians should've finished their day-to-day work by then, and it will mean overtime for them, so the answer will be yes!'

It was Crofts' turn to chuckle, as Snowy had hit the nail on the head. 'Funny how the prospect of overtime changes things. Let me know if there's a problem. Can you also get some undertakers on standby for when we've finished with the body at the scene?'

'Certainly. Do you know roughly what time?'

'I imagine it'll be around three. That should give us long enough.'

'Okey-doke, will do. I will inform the coroner, and if there's anything else you need doing, let me know,' Snowy finished.

Crofts thanked him and finished the call before turning to Hannah and Leighton, who were waiting to start the scene examination.

'Right, let's get to work,' Crofts told them. 'Due to the nature of the scene, I don't want to get involved with the rest of the building now. The most important thing today is to forensicate the body and then get it to the mortuary for the PM. The outcome of that will dictate how much more work we'll have to do at the scene.'

He deliberately used the word 'forensicate'. It was made up by police officers as a way of asking SOCOs to do a full job at a scene without describing the actions. Crofts and other SOCOs hated it at first, but he had come to like it and found it an easy way to refer to their work.

'It's all been photographed fully,' said Crofts, 'so we'll take swabs and tapings in situ, and then we can remove the body from the scene.'

The two SOCOs nodded in agreement and started to get the equipment needed. Crofts was as pleased as always that he had staff who knew what they were doing; it made everything so much easier for him.

He moved towards the body, carefully using the stepping plates to avoid disturbing any shoeprints on the floor. The first thing to do was to recover the syringe sticking out of the victim's arm. This would need checking for both fingerprints and DNA.

He and his team were experienced enough to carry out those examinations at the scene themselves, but Crofts decided it would be recovered and packaged there and then and sent to the forensic recovery unit in Guildford. This had been set up several years ago when the Sussex and Surrey forensic units had merged. The whole process was sold to everyone as progress, but they all knew it was to save money.

What it did mean, though, was that there were the facilities to carry out these types of examinations in controlled laboratory conditions. Crofts had looked around at the state of the scene and decided he would prefer the examination to be done at the FRU rather than here.

Leighton gingerly picked up the syringe, touching just the edges in an area that wouldn't yield fingerprints or DNA and placed it into the safety of a knife tube, held out by Hannah. This container comprised two clear plastic tubes which fitted into each other and could be twisted together and tightened until they were fully sealed. To make sure the syringe couldn't move around at all, a metal disc was inserted inside at the needle end. This meant that when the tube was tightened, it would stop that sharp point from protruding through the plastic, something that potentially could be very dangerous.

Once secured, the tube was put into a seal-fast bag, which was immediately signed and sealed. This was one of the most important parts of the process for the recovery of exhibits, and it was another thing Crofts had spent the last few years trying to teach officers to do. In the past, exhibits were often taken from scenes and then sealed back at the police station. But the whole process of exhibit handling had been brought into question when defence barristers started to query the practice and to intimate to juries that exhibits had been tampered with. Nowadays, every item was signed and sealed at the scene to avoid cases being lost.

Leighton then swabbed all the exposed areas of the body to recover any DNA left behind by anyone who had been in contact with the victim. He took swabs from around the face and neck, areas of potential DNA, especially since there had been some type of assault, and then continued to the hands and arms.

Next, he collected fingernail scrapings from the victim, another area where any assailant's DNA could end up. The

SOCOs then recovered tapings from all areas of the body, using strips of adhesive tape to lift any hairs and fibres from the victim's skin and pick up any loose fibres on the clothing.

This could potentially prove that a suspect had been involved with the victim, even when no DNA was found. All this evidence recovery took a long time. As well as packaging, signing and sealing every item, they had to record everything on the laptop, which added to the amount of time needed at the scene.

'How come you are taking so long?' was a question the SOCOs were used to hearing, and it was hard to explain to someone who was unaware of the process.

It was another thing Crofts would mention when giving talks, comparing their work with the television programmes that were able to show a crime, the investigation and the outcome in under an hour. In real life, SOCOs could spend that long just fibre-taping a sofa.

Not too glamorous.

Crofts checked his watch; it was two thirty already. The work was just about finished, and they only needed to bag the body, so he gave Snowy a call to tell him to get the undertakers en route. Crofts knew there was usually an hour's estimated time of arrival given, so that should work out fine.

Hannah and Leighton had laid a large plastic sheet on the floor beside the body. The three of them got hold of the victim and lifted him onto the body sheet. As he had been an addict, he was thin and undernourished, so he was easy to move.

This was not always the case. They had had problems in the past moving bodies due to their weight or size, or even because of where the body had been located. How his staff didn't have more back problems Crofts would never know. A dead body was a dead weight, and no amount of training in how to lift properly could help in certain situations.

Once the body was on the sheet, they fitted bags to the head, hands and feet to recover any evidence that was dislodged during transit. As the team had recovered a lot of evidence from these areas already, some would say this wasn't needed, but Crofts preferred to make sure.

The body sheet was wrapped around and twisted at the ends until they were left with a large, cracker-shaped object. The SOCOs wound tape around the twisted areas until they were secure and lifted the middle and wound tape around it to completely secure the package. They lifted it into a body bag, zipped it up, fastened on a label, and gave it an exhibit number.

Someone somewhere below in the building called out that the undertaker had arrived. Crofts made his way down to meet him at the edge of the cordon. It was a chap Crofts had met before. He didn't know his name but greeted him warmly.

The undertaker was dressed in the uniform of their profession: a smart black suit, white shirt and black tie. Something about undertakers made them stand out in a crowd, Crofts thought – not just the clothing but their comportment. He imagined they lived quiet, respectful lives, and this came over when working with them.

Crofts explained that the premises were too dangerous to go in, and as the body was bagged, he would take the undertaker's trolley and collect the body and bring it down. The undertaker was obviously relieved to not have to go into the building and happily handed over the foldable trolley for Crofts to use.

Once Crofts had returned to the others, they laid the body on the trolley and tightened the straps that held it in place. Bodies had been known to fall off trolleys if not secured correctly. Now came the fun and games of getting it down the stairs. The three of them worked as a team, talking each other through the obstacles along the route. It was dangerous: if one of them placed a foot in the wrong place, they could all end up falling through the floorboards or stairs, together with a dead body on a trolley. Not something any of them wanted.

They eventually reached the front door, lifted the trolley onto the path and wheeled it out to the undertaker who was now joined by another. As he handed it over to them, Crofts saw the flash of cameras. The local paparazzi were already on the case. He wondered where they got the information from, but the press was always there whatever the crime. Crofts often joked that he was photographed more times than some media stars, except that you couldn't always tell it was him under the coveralls and masks.

Once the undertakers had gone, the three SOCOs left the scene and took their kit off by their vans. Crofts told Hannah and Leighton to stop at a shop on the way to the mortuary. 'Remember that getting a packet of biscuits for the morticians usually means they'll offer us a cup of tea,' Crofts reminded them. He then drove off to the railway station to pick up the pathologist.

CHAPTER ELEVEN

Bethany had spent most of her life in and around the pub trade, so was aware that the success or failure of most establishments had everything to do with keeping the customers happy. She couldn't remember who it was who'd said it to her first, but the adage of 'the customer is always right' had been drilled into her over the years, and she always kept it at the forefront of her mind.

The fact that she was so introverted normally might have been a problem for her. However, she had enjoyed serving customers from a young age, and these days with her make-up to hide behind, she almost felt like an actress on stage. Which was how she approached it when she went to a table to introduce herself.

It was for this reason that some of the other staff didn't like her, especially the girls. They saw how she was with the customers – full of chat, fun and laughter – and wondered why she was so quiet with them. The main problem was that most of the girls were local and had grown up together, so knew each other really well. An outsider was always going to find it hard to fit in, and for someone slightly different it was definitely going to be a challenge. The one thing the other members of staff did know was that Bethany was a good worker, so they didn't say too much about her, especially since Sandy thought the world of her.

They had tried to invite her out on girlie nights, but Bethany always had a reason not to come. The yearly staff do that Malcolm and Sandy arranged after the Christmas rush, which had a James Bond theme that year. Everyone had gone except Bethany. Nobody believed the excuse she gave, that she had a virus, especially as she hadn't had a day off sick from work.

There was, however, a group of people who really did like Bethany, and they were the regular customers at The Moorings; in fact, they loved her.

During the daytime most of the customers were part of the blue-rinse brigade. They came a couple of times a week, so had got to know her well. A couple of the old ladies had christened her Cleo because of her make-up, saying she looked like a young Elizabeth Taylor, and the nickname had stuck amongst her fans.

Bethany was also liked because she paid attention to the customers, always remembered their names, and knew their likes and dislikes, which made them feel like royalty. Her attitude was different to that of some of the other young people, who were only there for the money, especially as some of them had no patience with older people. The customers soon picked up on that.

Two of Bethany's favourites had been in today, a pair of lovely eighty-year-old twin sisters who had an endearing habit of finishing each other's sentences, which meant that most of their conversations ended in giggles.

They always ordered the same food, which of course Bethany remembered. Soup starter, no bread roll, followed by cod in a cheese sauce ('Just a small piece of cod, please'), followed by one scoop of lemon sorbet each. People often wondered how the pub could sell food so cheaply. Little did they know senior citizens such as these two helped create the profit margins.

Bethany didn't know their names, nor did anyone else in the restaurant. Everyone just called them 'the twins', but they loved being served by Bethany and always tipped her well.

Nobody knew where they lived or where they went during the rest of the week, but they turned up every Monday lunchtime, always well dressed to enjoy their weekly trip to their favourite restaurant.

Bethany wished there were more customers like them. Unfortunately, it came with the territory that there were some customers who treated her as if she were the lowest of the low. It didn't bother her and she continued to be as nice to people as possible.

This was the life for her, and she was happy to put up with the rudeness if it meant she was able to continue to earn money from something she loved doing.

CHAPTER TWELVE

The journey down south had been easier than expected. The main motorways were as clear as possible, something that was unusual.

Stevie had figured out that some days he spent longer in traffic queues than he did working, but that was one of the pitfalls of being a sales rep. There weren't many other things he didn't like about it. As Freddie had told him, he was a natural for the sales world, with his easy-going, friendly nature, backed by an understanding of how to clinch a deal.

It had surprised Stevie himself.

Once they had moved into Moses Farm and Suzie had started to act like the lady of the manor, he had gone along for the sales training, which he'd excelled at, coming top of the class. He had then been given the obligatory Audi, and he had hit the road, his success continuing, with the added bonus that he also enjoyed it.

It did mean Stevie was on the road most weeks, but that didn't bother him. The problems between him and Suzie seemed to be eased the less they saw of each other. He had also learnt to put his time away to good use and organised everything whilst on the road, meaning they could have fun at weekends.

Once the twins had arrived, this slowly changed, as she relied on Stevie to cope with them all weekend. Luckily, he really enjoyed that too.

This week he was travelling down to Sussex, somewhere he had visited as a child on holiday with his grandparents. He had never visited for work so was looking forward to some good sales this week. The fact that this was an area with a large population of older people meant there was always a need for pharmaceuticals.

Stevie was aiming for Eastbourne, where he had booked a Travelodge for the first night, before moving on to Kent the following night. Travelodge wasn't top of the list of hotels for most reps, but Stevie had worked out early in his career that the expenses offered for overnight stays were easy to manage, and that since he was happy to stay in lesser hotels, he could make even more money. Something he needed, as Suzie's shopping habits had not changed. In fact, she had got worse since the twins were born, spending even more money on designer labels for them as well as for her.

After checking into the hotel a lot earlier than normal, Stevie decided to put the time to good use. He had an old acquaintance who ran a care home in nearby Bexhill and had already arranged to go and see him that afternoon. It was only an eight mile drive, so he got over there quickly and was ringing the bell around four o'clock in the afternoon. The assistant who answered the door started telling him they wouldn't talk to cold-calling reps when Stevie butted in and said he had an appointment with Dan Nicholls, the owner. That changed her attitude completely, and she asked him to wait while she found out where Dan was.

Stevie looked around at his surroundings. It was obviously

a better class of care home, though it had a strong ammonia smell of urine, but the decoration and furnishings were good quality. There were so many bad-quality homes Stevie had visited that it made him feel good inside when he came to one like this. He also knew that the cost of staying here would be a lot higher.

Dan arrived and welcomed him enthusiastically. They had been introduced by Freddie originally, so there would be plenty to discuss about Freddie's latest exploits.

Dan took Stevie into his large, plush office off to one side of the reception area. One of Dan's young assistants brought in a cafetière of coffee and some fancy biscuits. Stevie could tell by the body language that she was more than just an assistant, a fact that Dan spotted, as it was a bit too obvious, but he carried on as if nothing had happened. Stevie was polite enough to ignore it; Dan was a big player in the care home business in this part of the country, owning six large complexes. What the man did in his private life didn't interest Stevie; he just wanted the sale.

The next half hour was taken up by talk of Freddie before Dan got on to his favourite subject: Dan. Stevie had soon learnt that one of the skills needed by a good salesman is the ability to listen. So, Stevie politely listened to everything Dan was telling him, waiting for the moment he could start to introduce the subject he was there for.

It took a while, but they eventually got on to drugs and suppliers, and Stevie smoothly went into his sales pitch without Dan even realising it. In fact, Stevie had got so good at slipping the patter into conversation that some clients didn't notice at all.

Dan was a little more experienced than that, but Stevie could tell he liked what he was saying. He also knew he was offering a good rate, undercutting Dan's normal suppliers, and so the deal was struck. Even better, it was a deal for all six care home complexes Dan owned, so it was a win-win for both parties.

They shook hands and arranged a social meeting including wives in the future, although Stevie knew it would never happen. Suzie wouldn't want anything to do with anyone from the healthcare world.

After they said their goodbyes, Stevie drove off happy. He knew his forward planning had helped again.

Many reps would have arrived in the afternoon, booked into their hotel, eaten and waited until the next day before even thinking about work. He had got in early, made money from expenses and then sealed a deal which would have been good enough for a week's commission for some, but not for Stevie.

That was why he was so successful, he thought, as he drove towards the seafront to find somewhere to park up. Stevie wanted to speak to the twins before their bedtime.

CHAPTER THIRTEEN

Crofts spotted the tall, gangly figure of Andrew Eaton as soon as he appeared on the platform and hailed him over.

Eaton climbed into the car and thanked Crofts for picking him up.

By the time Crofts had updated Eaton about the job they had arrived at Hastings' Conquest Hospital. As with most hospitals, the mortuary was hidden from view, down a side road away from the main body of the building.

Crofts pressed the buzzer, knowing he was on camera in the office.

'Come in, darling!' replied a loud voice, which Crofts knew belonged to chief mortuary technician, Linda Pearce.

He smiled apologetically to Andrew Eaton, who cringed and rolled his eyes. Crofts had met many morticians all over the country, but Linda was one of the loudest, and jolliest; two attributes that Crofts knew Eaton didn't enjoy.

They entered the mortuary, which was the usual white and smelt the same as they all did. Crofts could never put his finger on what the smell actually was, but he put it down to a mixture of disinfectant and dead and decaying bodies. It was like no other.

Linda had already popped her head out of the office and was welcoming Doctor Eaton as loudly and exuberantly as ever. Crofts couldn't tell whether she realised he didn't like her, but it wouldn't matter to her anyway.

Mortuary technicians had to be made of strong stuff, thick-skinned and able to deal with all eventualities. Crofts had seen them in action at post-mortems. Whether with burnt or maggot-infested bodies, old people or young children or babies, they always carried out their tasks professionally. Minutes after a post-mortem they could be looking after a grieving relative who had come to identify their dead family member in the chapel of rest.

Crofts had known Linda from the first days of becoming a SOCO. They were of a similar age, and they had the added connection of having children of the same age, so they got on well. He knew he could trust Linda to do her job efficiently, which was another thing for him not to worry about.

Hannah and Leighton had already arrived, together with Snowy, each with a coffee and what appeared to be an empty plate, having eaten most of the biscuits they brought with them. Ali West, the other mortuary assistant, saw the look on Crofts' face and offered him a cup of tea, which he readily accepted, realising he hadn't eaten or drunk since early morning.

He checked with the two SOCOs that all the kit was ready and made the decision that Hannah would act as photographer during the PM and Leighton would be on exhibit packaging. It didn't really matter with the two he had today, as both had similar experience. In fact, they had started on the same day. Also, in this case Hannah had taken most of the photographs at the scene, so it would be easier for her to continue, making it simpler when the case came to court.

Once everyone had had a drink and a chance to use the loo, they prepared themselves for the PM. The SOCOs wore their full PPE; the morticians and the pathologist wore scrubs with plastic aprons and white wellies to finish off their outfits.

Tom Mead and Alison Williams chose that moment to arrive. On the drive over, the decision had been made that they would watch the PM from the viewing gallery, a small room overlooking the main examination area, so they wouldn't need to wear PPE (or put up with the smell). It also made things easier for the two detectives because mobile phones could be used freely from there without annoying everyone in the PM room.

The SIO and his deputy had lots of other lines of enquiry to keep an eye on whilst the PM took place. It also made things easier for the SOCOs, as there would be more room during the PM. The forensic strategy that Mead and Crofts agreed earlier that morning would be used, so everyone was well aware of what was needed. The detectives made their way into the viewing gallery and were joined by Snowy, whilst everyone else walked round to the PM room.

CHAPTER FOURTEEN

Stevie pulled the car over near to the seafront at Bexhill and called home on his iPhone. It took a while for Suzie to answer, and when she did, he could tell she wasn't happy. She soon explained that the twins had been grizzly all day, which would have been bad enough normally, but it was also the day Suzie had decided to take them to a play area in the town centre to meet up with another designer mummy, Michelle. She had a daughter, Ebony, the same age as the twins, and they normally played well together. However, today had been a nightmare, as none of them had wanted to play at all. Rather than feel sorry for the twins who were ill, Suzie was embarrassed by the whole episode, and she left Michelle and Ebony on their own, Michelle vowing never to meet up with her ever again.

Stevie listened and made the right sounds but really wasn't that interested. All he wanted was to see the twins. He waited for a significant pause and then butted in, asking Suzie to put FaceTime on.

'Oh sure,' she replied. 'You're not interested in me anymore, are you?' Without giving Stevie time to reply, she continued: 'You go away all the time, leaving me to bring up the twins, which is bloody hard work. You then call and all you want to do is talk to them. Same as at the weekend when you eventually get home, it's all about them, not me. I've had enough!'

It was an argument they constantly had. He tried to calm her down by reminding her that he had to work away all the time to make them money. He then told her about the contract he had won that day, which placated her a little.

'When you get home, we need to speak about this again,' she said. 'I can't cope on my own. You need to see if Freddie can find you something more local, so you can work from home.'

Stevie said that he would speak to Freddie, knowing he wouldn't. One of the reasons he enjoyed his job so much was that it got him away from her.

She agreed to switch to FaceTime and within seconds had set the phone up so they could see each other. He called the twins' names, causing them to stop what they were doing and look at where Daddy's voice was coming from. He was sure their little faces lit up when they heard him, which made him feel guilty. Maybe he did need to rethink his options after all.

Stevie spent the next couple of minutes smiling and calling to the twins, who did the same back. The conversation was only interrupted briefly, when an old woman walking her little dog stared at him through the car window. He couldn't care less. This was the best moment of his day, and he didn't mind who was watching.

He could see the twins were getting bored, so he called out to Suzie, who eventually turned up. The expression on her face told him she wasn't happy that she was now back in charge, so to speak. She said a stroppy goodbye and switched the connection off.

Stevie sat staring at the empty screen for a few moments, wishing there was a way to whisk his babies away from Suzie, but not sure how. He still had a lot of belief in himself and knew that something would work out soon.

It always had.

He decided he would treat himself to fish and chips tonight, as he was by the seaside, and drove off along the coast road through Cooden Beach to Normans Bay. This was a place that held great memories for him.

When he was little, his nan and granddad used to sometimes take him there in the summer holidays in their caravan. It was perfect for kids, a campsite that was next to the beach, somewhere to make sandcastles, dig holes in the sand to bury granddad and to play pirates. The evening show in the clubhouse was maybe what had drawn him into his early life as an entertainer.

Stevie knew that in nearby Pevensey Bay there were plenty of takeaways, and that was where he was headed. Driving along the potholed, unadopted road, he wondered if it would ever be tarmacked properly – he could still hear his granddad moaning about it from all those years ago.

Stevie drove past the tents and caravans, with children playing outside, and a warm glow went through him as the memories of his childhood returned. The strange thing was that the site looked exactly as he recalled.

As usual when travelling, he had tuned in to a local radio station, mainly to keep up to date with traffic news. In this area it was Sovereign FM, a commercial station with more adverts than music. Half listening, the advert for The Moorings ('The pub on the beach') caught his attention when it mentioned all three-course meals were only ten pounds. He made a mental note to check it out, then pulled up as the traffic slowed to a stop for roadworks.

There were essential gas repairs going on. The queue was half a mile long, but there was no point in turning back, as it was a long way around. It took him twenty minutes to shuffle forward, but at last he could see the temporary traffic lights. He also saw a sign announcing that The Moorings was on the next turning left.

Stevie had a feeling it would make a nice change and turned left down towards the pub. He drove along a small residential street and at the end into a car park that was on the beach itself. Finding a space, he parked up.

On climbing out of the car, he turned and got his first view of The Moorings, and it was good. It was a large, detached building on the edge of the beach. Over the years it had expanded, and there were now large areas of conservatory at the front, overlooking the sea. In the evening sunlight, the tables and chairs outside looked inviting. Stevie believed he was just about to cap a perfect day.

CHAPTER FIFTEEN

The post-mortem commenced with Andrew Eaton asking who would be handing the body to him, as part of the chain of evidence. This was very important, since it could, in some circumstances, lead to the wrong body being examined. In this case, it was Snowy, as he had met the undertakers outside the scene and had then followed them to the mortuary.

As soon as the body was identified, Hannah started taking photos. First, the full body bag, and then it being unzipped, and each stage after. She moved around while taking the images, at times using a small stepladder, always making sure that someone was holding it secure. SOCOs had been known to fall onto the body they were photographing whilst concentrating on their camera and forgetting they were high up.

The two mortuary technicians took each layer of the packaging off, one at a time, and handed them to Crofts, who put them in a brown paper evidence bag. Once they got to the body, Eaton started a commentary into a voice recorder, describing the victim's clothing. As each item was mentioned, it was taken off by the morticians, photographed and exhibited.

Once the body was fully unclothed and photographed,

Eaton went over every inch of the skin, recording every blemish, scar, bruise and, in this case, needle mark. Sometimes he would call for close-ups of something of particular interest, meaning Hannah had to keep changing lenses between the macro and the standard. She was very experienced at this and made it look easy. She had also connected a ring flash, which gave a constant circle of light around the lens and excluded any shadows on the images.

Eaton then looked carefully at the head injuries that Crofts had noticed at the scene. Once he had cleaned them up, they only appeared superficial, and apart from photographing and recording them, there was nothing more to note. All part and parcel of living on the streets.

Whilst Hannah and the pathologist were busy, Crofts and Leighton continued to package every item, labelling as they went. Eaton dissected the arm around where the needle had been found and took samples. He then asked what swabs were required. The majority of the touch DNA work had been done at the scene, so only sex swabs of the genital and anal areas were needed. At this stage of the enquiry, no one could tell what allegations the suspects may throw up, and the fact that sex in any form could be a reason for the death dictated that these should be taken now.

Once Eaton was satisfied he had everything recorded and swabbed, the morticians turned the deceased over and he repeated the process on the back of the body. Once that was finished, the body was turned again, and Eaton took hold of his scalpel and commenced the internal examination.

He cut a large V-shape in the chest. This enabled him to access the ribs, and these were then cut out too. It was at this moment that the smell in the mortuary changed. All involved in this case were experienced and were ready for it, but anyone attending a post-mortem for the first time would get caught out.

The mortuary already had an unusual smell. Once the body was cut open and the stench of the decomposing internal organs escaped, this intensified. Always different depending on the age and condition of the body, it was an odour that Crofts found impossible to describe. And even though this body was less than twenty-four hours cold, the conditions that it had been left in meant the effect was very strong.

Over the years, Crofts had heard loads of supposed ways of dealing with these smells, from putting vapour rub up the nose, to sucking menthol sweets, but in his mind none of them worked. In one case, a DC who had sucked on a particularly strong menthol cough sweet actually cleared his nose so well that he ended up smelling the body stench even better.

Crofts knew that some of the odour was kept out by his mask, but it was still there. He had learnt to put up with it by breathing through his mouth, and it didn't bother him.

Eaton cut free and removed the whole set of internal organs. It never ceased to amaze Crofts how easy it was to remove most of a person's insides in one movement. It showed how simple the human body was, but at the same time how complicated.

Eaton put the internal organs on a chopping board and started to work on them, weighing and minutely inspecting each organ for any imperfections. These could show the cause of death was natural, and this had to be ruled out before they went any further. Eaton then sliced through each organ, again looking for unnatural flaws.

As with many people who had been living on the streets, a lot of the victim's organs were less healthy than those of other people of the same age, so Eaton again had to rule this out as the cause of death. This took some time, but he finished the examinations and took small samples for histology, before moving back to the remains of the body on the slab.

Eaton started to dissect the neck area. He was checking for

bruising and to see if the hyoid was damaged. This was a small horseshoe-shaped bone in the neck area. If the victim had been strangled, it would have been broken. He also noted the absence of any petechial haemorrhage around the eyes and lips. This was another factor which might have proven strangulation.

In this particular case, one of the most important results would be the level of drugs in the body. This could be established using blood or urine in a living person but wasn't quite as simple in a dead body. Firstly, in some cases the victim may have lost so much blood from a wound, for instance, that there wasn't much left. Also, the blood may have been contaminated by other bodily fluids, and the same could happen with urine. So, vitreous humor – the fluid in the eye – was also taken.

Eaton recovered a sample using a syringe and handed it to Crofts to package. He then asked the morticians to lift one of the deceased's legs and cut through the femoral artery to recover some blood. This was successful, and they were able to get a jar full of blood, which Crofts took over to the sink and decanted into two smaller bottles, one for drugs and alcohol levels and one for DNA. Eaton then cut into the bladder and recovered a sample of urine.

Eaton declared that the PM was finished and said he would meet the SIO and Crofts in the office to discuss his findings. Crofts reminded the two SOCOs to fingerprint the body before leaving. The prints would not only be used as elimination prints for items found at the scene, but they would also be used to remove the victim's name from the national fingerprint system.

The morticians had already begun skilfully sewing the body up to make it look as undamaged as possible for when relatives came to identify the deceased.

By the time Crofts disrobed and walked round to the office, the others were already there. He could tell just by looking at her that Alison Williams had not enjoyed the PM, even though she was watching behind a glass screen in a different room. Crofts guessed she hadn't been to many in the past.

Eaton slowly went through all the reasons that the death hadn't been from natural causes and explained that none of the minor injuries on the body would have caused the victim to die. He concluded that the cause of death was unknown at this stage and would depend on the results of toxicology. Crofts refrained from saying that he could have told him that hours ago. Instead, he arranged to meet the SIO in the morning to discuss what was needed at the scene.

Everyone said their goodbyes, and Crofts took Eaton back to the station. It was now nearly nine o'clock at night, but Eaton was happy he would make it back home okay. In fact, he was quite chatty on the way, something Crofts wasn't ready for. As always after attending a post-mortem, he felt a bit down, probably because it reminded him of his own mortality, so he could have done without the chatter. He supposed that for Eaton it was a way of letting off steam.

After dropping Eaton off at the station, Crofts went back to the office in Eastbourne. It was dark again as he drove, and he realised he had been up since three and had been on the go for eighteen hours. All the time he had been doing something, he hadn't noticed the tiredness, but now that the end was in sight, he could feel it trying to catch him up.

Driving in the dark didn't help, so he turned the radio to TalkSPORT to try to keep his concentration. While he listened to the chat about football, he drove past the sign to Pevensey Bay, which reminded him that Oscar's football team were playing Pevensey and Westham FC on Sunday. This cheered him up; football was one of his escapes from the stress of his job, and he looked forward to those games.

Hannah and Leighton were already at the office when he

arrived and were busy sorting out the exhibits and making sure all information on the computer system was updated. This would take them at least another hour or so, as everything had to be in place before they went off duty in case anyone needed to check any details overnight.

Leighton was already on the phone to a local pizza delivery company. 'Do you want one?' he asked Crofts.

Crofts declined, saying that he was just leaving and would rather get home and eat. He knew he wasn't on call that night so might even have a glass of red with it, if he could stay awake long enough.

He scanned through his emails, and then booked himself off duty.

'Hey, you two, can you stop for a minute? I need a word,' he called to Leighton and Hannah.

He gave them a small debrief, reminding them that what they had been dealing with today was not nice and that they may experience flashbacks in the next day or so. This was a normal reaction, but if they still found themselves dwelling on things after forty-eight hours, they needed to speak to him to arrange a debriefing session. This would be done with trained counsellors if required.

Neither Hannah nor Leighton thought they would need anything like that on this job, but they thanked Crofts anyway. He told them not to take too long, as it had been a long day for them too. It was ten in the evening by the time he headed out of the door. Another long day, but nothing unusual. He jumped on his bicycle for the short journey home.

CHAPTER SIXTEEN

Bethany spotted Stevie Johnson as soon as he walked in for two reasons. Firstly, being her usual efficient self, she had already made sure that all her customers were dealt with and had been served their main courses, so she had a lull in proceedings. Secondly, it was unusual for someone to come into the restaurant on their own. Most who visited were couples or groups. Bethany walked over to the waiting area as soon as she could.

'Hi there. Do you have a table for one tonight?' he asked.

Bethany knew exactly how many covers they had that evening, told him straight away that there was room for him and led him to a table in the conservatory overlooking the beach. He ordered a pint of bitter shandy, due to the fact that he was driving he told her. She showed him the menu and told him the daily specials, then went away to collect the drink.

Stevie browsed the menu, unable to believe the prices. There were varied starters, main courses of everything from steaks and fish to pies, and then desserts, all for ten pounds. No wonder the place was busy on a Monday night, a night most restaurants dreaded and, in some cases, didn't even bother opening on.

Stevie had already decided that his initial fancy of fish and chips was still what he wanted, especially as it was locally caught cod, his favourite. Bethany returned with his drink, and for the first time he really noticed her. He couldn't decide whether she was trying to look like Siouxsie Sioux from the punk band Siouxsie and The Banshees. It was one of his favourite groups, but then he realised her age and thought better of asking, as she probably wouldn't know who he was talking about. Whatever, there was something intriguing about her.

Bethany smiled pleasantly as she took Stevie's order and when he told her that he'd never been to the pub before.

He ordered the Camembert with plum sauce as a starter followed by cod and chips. Bethany didn't write down the simple order, just nodded and smiled again before going back to the kitchen.

Stevie sat back and enjoyed the view. It was starting to get dark outside and the vista changed as he watched, clouds moving and the colours of the sky fluctuating as the sun slowly set. He was looking east, so the reflective glow gave him a free light show. He started to think about his life and future. There was no way he could continue with Suzie, but he couldn't live without the twins.

He wondered, as he often did lately, whether she would give him custody of them if they split.

His thoughts were interrupted by Bethany arriving with the starter.

'Blimey, that was quick!' Stevie exclaimed.

Bethany blushed a little. She wasn't used to dealing with confident middle-aged men like Stevie, as most of her customers were old and genteel. She explained that the chefs were very good at their job and prided themselves on how quickly they could prepare their starters. She told him to enjoy the meal and left with a smile.

Stevie tucked in, as he was ravenous, realising that he had only eaten a couple of biscuits during the day. The Camembert was good, with a side salad and a small dish of sauce; just what was needed. His thoughts again turned to the twins and what he could do in the future. As usual in his life, he had taken on a new challenge and had been successful. He knew he would be able to bring up the twins on his own. The type of work he did meant that he could take a sidestep into something similar with more stable hours if he wanted to, and if he didn't have to pay for Suzie's upkeep.

Again, his thoughts were interrupted by Bethany, who had come over to clear his plate and to reset his place for the main course. Stevie thanked her and was about to return to his thoughts when Bethany arrived back at the table carrying a plate with one of the largest pieces of cod he had ever seen overhanging the rim, with chips piled either side. Teetering on the edge was a small bowl of mushy peas.

'Wow!' exclaimed Stevie. 'That is impressive. I'm not sure I'll be able to eat all of that!'

Bethany smiled. 'I must admit, a lot of customers say that when it arrives, but I'm sure you'll be fine once you've tasted it.'

'Is that a challenge?' he asked, with a friendly smile.

'That's up to you,' Bethany replied, blushing again. 'Enjoy your meal,' she added, before busying herself with another table next to her. She hated blushing like that and knew that the make-up covered most of it, but he was a nice, friendly chap, and it caught her unawares.

As Stevie munched his way through the delicious cod, his thoughts returned to his and the twins' future. He wasn't sure if it was just the euphoria of the deal that day, or whether it was the childhood holiday memories, but he suddenly thought about moving away from his home town, maybe even to this area. It would be so much better for them to grow up in a seaside town on the south coast. It would feel like being on holiday permanently. Not as good as his younger days in the Balearics, but great for those lovely kiddies of his.

Stevie looked around the restaurant. All he could see were smiles and laughter. It was infectious, and he decided there and then on a plan. If it worked, he would get rid of Suzie, probably to her relief, and he would be free to move down to the south coast with the twins, get himself an office-hours job, get an au pair for during the day, and have every evening and every weekend with his children.

Mind made up, Stevie realised he had eaten all the food.

Bethany had spotted him and came over. 'I told you that you would finish it!' she said, smiling.

'That was absolutely lovely,' he replied. 'I can't believe I ate it all.'

'Now, you only have a dessert to finish off, and they're delicious too,' she replied as she handed him the menu.

Stevie had a quick glance and was about to say no when he spotted his favourite. 'I might as well completely pig out and have the banoffee pie then,' he replied, which made Bethany giggle.

'Would you like cream with that?'

'Oh my God, are you trying to kill me or something?'

Bethany was laughing now.

'Actually, no, I'm watching my weight,' he said with a deadpan expression.

Bethany laughed again and went off to the kitchen with the order.

Sandy had been watching the exchange and was pleased to see Bethany in that frame of mind, so went over to talk to the customer herself.

'Evening, sir, I hope you enjoyed your meal.'

'It was fantastic,' Stevie answered, 'and such good value for money. Are you the owner?'

Sandy replied that she was and started to tell him about the history of their business. Just then Bethany returned with a huge slab of banoffee pie and placed it on the table.

'You get off now, Bethany, so you can catch the bus,' said Sandy. 'You've had a long day, and thanks for your work. See you tomorrow.'

'Thanks,' she replied, and went off to get her jacket.

'She's a very good waitress,' Stevie observed. 'I was hoping to give her a tip.'

'Don't worry,' said Sandy. 'All tips are pooled here and paid out equally, so she'll get her share when she comes in tomorrow. We've always done it that way so that the kitchen staff get a share of the tips too, not just the waiting staff. All of them love the idea.'

'I'm sure they do,' said Stevie.

'Are you just visiting?' Sandy asked.

Stevie explained about his job and why he was there. He then went on to say that now he had been to this area, he would be returning, and that he was even thinking of moving down with his twins.

Sandy told him that she and Malcolm had moved down from London twenty years ago and they had never regretted it. They hadn't had children, as the business had been their baby, but she had plenty of friends who did have, and all of them loved the area. In fact, most of her staff were teenagers who had grown up locally, and she knew from talking to them over the years that they each realised how lucky they were.

Stevie knew then that it was what he wanted, and he also knew that when he wanted something he would make sure he got it. The future was looking rosy again. All he had to do was get rid of his bitch of a wife.

CHAPTER SEVENTEEN

People quite often asked Crofts why he cycled to and from work. Tonight was one of the reasons why. It was a warm night with a light breeze. He had put his headphones on and was listening to one of his favourites, Simple Minds playing 'Don't You (Forget About Me)', as he pedalled off. A quick halt at the gate to open the electronic exit and he was away. Onto a cycle path with the music playing; it was one of his ways to unwind. It was only just over a mile but at the same time gave him a small amount of exercise each day. He'd been an athletic young Royal Marine in his early life, and he knew he wasn't as fit as he could be anymore with his work commitments and family life, so every little helped.

He cycled through an industrial estate and then past the twenty-four-hour McDonald's, the car park filling up with the boy racers, who would spend the evening with music blaring out, admiring each other's cars, and every now and then daring to do some screeching handbrake turns. Next, the large Tesco came into view; this was also open twenty-four hours. It reminded him that his job wasn't the only one with unsociable hours. It was also handy for him and his staff to get all kinds of provisions at any time of the night, unlike when he first started the job and had had to wait until morning.

The klaxon sounded at the beginning of 'Waterfront', bringing a smile to his face. This was the song that he and his mates had known as their signature tune on their nights out in Union Street in Plymouth, and that would lead everyone onto the dance floor. What great times they were, and how different his life now was, but he wouldn't change either.

The smell from the KFC as he passed reminded him that he was hungry. Attending post-mortems always seemed to make him hungry. He had no idea why. (Not to mention, for some less experienced officers, attending a PM would put them off food for a day or two.) Luckily, Deborah had texted him earlier to say she had cooked a lasagne, one of his favourites, so he was willing to wait another few minutes. He cycled into the street he lived on. It felt uncanny that the street was as quiet as it had been when he left that morning. It seemed so long ago. Sometimes he went for weeks without seeing it during the day due to protracted jobs, although when he finally had a day off, he found that nothing much had happened anyway. He put his bike away in the garage and locked it up before letting himself in.

'Hello, darling,' Deborah called to him as he walked in, and then came over and gave him a kiss. 'You stink of the hospital! Before you do anything, there's someone waiting to see you.' She had a mock disapproving look on her face, which turned into a smile. 'He should be asleep by now on a school night, but he's waiting to tell you something.'

Crofts smiled and headed up the stairs to Oscar's bedroom. As he opened the door, he could just make out a big smile and big blue eyes through the darkness. Oscar was obviously eager to tell him his news.

'Dad, I scored two goals at football training tonight. One was a header!'

Crofts smiled and listened to the replay of both goals, every movement by each player remembered in detail by his football-mad son.

'That's great,' Crofts replied at the end of the second rerun. 'That'll get you ready for Sunday's cup match against Pevensey and Westham.'

'What have you been doing today, Dad?' was the next question, and one that he always hated, as it meant that he would have to lie to his son, something he didn't like doing.

'I've just been working on a job in Hastings. That's why I'm late. It took a long time to drive back.'

'Okay.'

'Come on now, it's time for sleep, you've school in the morning,' he said, adjusting the duvet and bending over to give his son a kiss goodnight. It was obviously all that was needed, as Oscar fell asleep with a smile on his face almost immediately.

Crofts had a quick shower and then went downstairs, where there was a bowl of home-made lasagne waiting for him with a nice glass of Merlot sitting next to it.

'Who could ask for a better wife?' Crofts asked as Deborah smiled and started updating him with what had happened that day at school, at her work and at football training.

As usual, there was plenty for her to talk about, and she was a bit of a chatterbox anyway, so Crofts let it all sink in whilst enjoying the lovely food. They talked about other things, and Crofts gave her a brief update on his day, albeit missing out most of the gruesome parts.

He helped himself to another glass of red before discussing their plans for the weekend, which he had off for a change. They had been invited to a BBQ on the Saturday night, and Oscar had a football match at twelve on the Sunday, which meant there was a chance of a lie-in, something of a rarity these days.

Crofts felt his weariness creeping up on him. The fact that he had been on the go for over twenty hours meant he felt exhausted now that he had finally sat down and relaxed. Deborah said she would sort out the dishes, so he went upstairs, cleaned his teeth, had a last check on the sleeping Oscar and was asleep before Deborah had even finished putting the plates in the dishwasher.

CHAPTER EIGHTEEN

Stevie walked out to his car and again marvelled at the location of the pub. He remembered coming to this area when he was a child with his grandparents, but he couldn't remember the actual pub. He would have to check through his childhood holiday snaps when he got home to see if there were any taken around that area. He wanted to bring the twins here; they would love it.

He jumped into his car, set up the satnav for the hotel and drove down the side street as directed. As he pulled out onto the main road towards Eastbourne, he saw someone standing at the bus stop. It was the waitress. She looked distressed, checking her phone and looking up the road in panic. He pulled over into the bus stop, wound down the window, and called out, 'Is everything okay?' She looked even more panicked, but then Stevie saw that she recognised who he was and calmed down a little.

'It looks like the last bus has been cancelled,' Bethany replied tearfully. 'It's happened before. There's no way of telling anyone, they just do it.'

'Do you need a lift?' Stevie asked.

'It's okay, I'll call a cab,' she replied a little too quickly.

Stevie suspected she was torn between the thought of waiting for a cab on her own and getting into a car with a stranger – neither was good for a young girl on her own. He tried again to be as friendly as possible, as he didn't want to leave her alone in the dark.

'Where do you live? I'm heading to the Travelodge on the seafront at Eastbourne. I can drop you anywhere on the way if that helps. I'm sorry, I don't know my way around this area.'

Bethany seemed to weigh up the suggestion. 'Okay, that would be nice. You can drop me off there, as I live just around the corner.'

'Great, jump in. I'm Stevie by the way, and there is honestly nothing to worry about. You can trust me.'

'Thanks. I'm Bethany,' she said as she got in.

As Bethany sat in the passenger seat, she almost started crying with relief. What she hadn't mentioned was that when the bus had been cancelled in the past, she had sometimes had to wait up to an hour for a taxi, in the dark on her own, and it really spooked her.

Stevie noticed how upset she was so decided to put her at ease by telling her about his time as a DJ in Ibiza, something he thought a youngster would be interested in. By luck he was right, as Bethany did like the dance music Stevie was talking about and had some of that type of music from that era downloaded on her phone. Slowly she started to relax as they travelled back to Eastbourne.

Bethany was genuinely impressed with Stevie's stories of the DJs he had met on the circuit during his day, and she couldn't believe Stevie knew them all. From the questions she asked, he could tell she really was interested in the subject and not just agreeing for the sake of it.

As they approached the seafront, and Stevie knew roughly

where he was, he again offered to take her to her flat, but she declined, saying he had done enough as it was.

He found a parking space near the hotel. Over the road was a pub called the Crown and Anchor, advertising live music that night.

'Here,' Stevie said. 'Do you fancy a drink and listening to some music in there?'

'I'm not really into going out at this time of night,' Bethany replied.

'That's a shame. I'm only here for one night. I fancy a drink but don't fancy going out on my own.'

Bethany felt a little worried. This wasn't something she would normally be doing. She wasn't used to being out with men in general. This guy seemed such a nice man, and he had given her a lift back to town but she wasn't sure.

'It's known as "Messy Monday" in town on a Monday night, as lots of the pubs give drink deals to attract the students, so it'll be packed full of drunken teenagers,' she replied, trying to let him down gently.

'Sorry. I've just realised you wouldn't want your friends to see you with this ageing DJ!' Stevie said lightly.

'I don't have any friends,' Bethany blurted out a little too quickly.

'You are joking,' he replied, genuinely surprised. 'I thought that someone as lovely looking as you would have loads of friends.'

'No,' she replied.

'In that case, I demand that you come for a drink with me. There'll be no one in there who knows either of us, so who gives a shit?' Stevie replied with a big smile on his face.

Bethany knew she was beaten. Stevie seemed a genuine type of guy, so she finally agreed.

When they entered the pub, no one took any notice of them,

as they were all watching the group performing at one end of the bar. Stevie noticed that the clientele were of all ages and walks of life, not just students, and that everyone appeared to be having a good time, and he pointed this out to Bethany before asking her what she wanted to drink. She said she wanted a fruit cider so he attracted the attention of one of the pretty barmaids. All were wearing the same pub T-shirt with the logo *'I've been Crown and Anchored'*.

Stevie asked for a cider and was told that it was two for one, as it was a Monday night, so he said yes to that before ordering a pint of Stella for himself. It was served in one of the Stella Artois glasses with a stem and looked very inviting indeed.

Bethany took a sip of her drink as Stevie took a deep slug of his lager. It was probably because of the fish and chips, but he suddenly felt thirsty and finished it in quick time, ordering another for the two of them. The band had stopped for a break, so they could finally talk and be heard.

'I can't believe this,' he said. 'Normally by now I would be tucked up in bed in the nearest Travelodge reading a book, trying to get some sleep. Today I've had a lovely meal, come to a great pub with a nice atmosphere, and am drinking with an attractive young lady. What could be better?'

Bethany smiled back. He really was a nice guy, and she was warming to him. Although he wasn't her type and was obviously too old for her, it didn't matter; for the first time in ages she was enjoying herself. She wasn't even worried about people looking at her, as everyone was having too good a time to bother.

The band started playing again. Picking up on the atmosphere of the audience, they started to belt out numbers that everyone could join in with. The mood was catching. As each old favourite started, more people joined in, and by the time they came back for their encore – which, to no one's surprise, was 'Hi Ho Silver Lining' – the whole crowd and the bar staff were singing and dancing together.

Stevie couldn't remember the last time he had had such a great night. Whenever it was, it was before he met Suzie, he thought, and laughed out loud.

One of the bar staff called out 'Last orders at the bar' just as the music finished. He had drunk plenty of Stella by then, so asked for two shots of sambuca instead. He took them over to Bethany and they raised their glasses for a toast to a great night. As everyone was making their weary way out of the pub, Stevie and Bethany followed.

Outside the main door, Bethany suddenly grabbed Stevie's arm to steady herself. 'Oh God, I don't feel too well,' she slurred.

It was the first night out drinking alcohol she'd had for many months, and she had drunk quite a lot. The world was spinning. Stevie was feeling a little tipsy as well but managed to hold on to her to stop her from falling. He asked her how far it was to her flat, but she just smiled and lurched to one side again.

Since they were only across the road from the Travelodge, Stevie decided to take her there, so she could have a sit down and a coffee to sober up. As usual at this time of night in these places, there was nobody at the reception desk. He got her into the lift and then along the corridor to his room.

As Bethany was so petite, he had no problems carrying her and lying her down on the bed. He put the kettle on and asked her whether she wanted a coffee, but all he got in reply was snoring. Stevie smiled and made himself a coffee, remembering he was working in the morning. Having flicked through most of the TV channels, he decided to instead let house music flood the room. Once he had finished his coffee, he went to the bathroom and cleaned his teeth. He turned the lights off and stripped down to his boxers and started to climb in under the duvet.

Bethany was still fully clothed on top of the bedding, and he thought he ought to cover her as well, so she didn't wake up cold in the night. As he lifted the bedding over her, in the dull light from the outside street lamps he noticed that her blouse was rucked up at the back, exposing a section of her small black lacy bra. In his drunken mind, he found it quite provocative. He lifted her blouse a little higher to get a better look, giggling to himself as if he were a naughty schoolboy. It really did look nice from behind, but that wasn't enough, and he now wanted to see how the front looked, so he gently rolled her over onto her back, slowly lifting the blouse as he did so. As he adjusted her blouse, Bethany let out a slight murmur, which Stevie thought of as a sound of contentment, so he slowly rolled one of his thumbs underneath the bra and let it caress her nipple. Bethany murmured again, which he decided meant that she was enjoying the experience. He continued with the other breast as well, by now fully aroused. He slipped his boxers down and took one of Bethany's hands and put it around his manhood, slowly thrusting into her grip. She looked so lovely lying there with that exotic make-up, her breasts exposed, playing with his penis. It was the perfect ending to a fabulous night.

Bethany had been completely out of it since they left the pub, but something in her brain made her wake up at that moment to find Stevie on top of her, groping her breasts whilst thrusting his penis against her. It was a horrible reminder of some of the sexual abuse she had to endure in children's homes over the years, which was probably what had triggered her mind and brought her round.

Whatever it was, she managed to say 'Stop!' before Stevie realised she was awake. He tried to kiss her, to stop her talking and so he could continue with what he was doing, as he was nearly at the end of his enjoyment. Bethany panicked as he covered her mouth with his. She grabbed hold of his balls and squeezed with all her might, digging her fingernails into the soft flesh.

'Bitch!' screamed Stevie as white-hot pain burst through his scrotum and awakened him from his drunken dreamworld. He let go of her breasts, and she let go of his parts at the same time. He kicked her away from him with both feet. The combination of his strength and his anger against her slight form meant that she flew across the bed. The momentum carried her over to the dressing table, and the back of her head hit the corner of it with a sickening thud. Bethany landed on the floor like a rag doll and didn't move again.

CHAPTER NINETEEN

Stevie rolled around in agony on the bed, not realising what he had just done. He called Bethany every name under the sun; he couldn't believe what she had done to him. The dance music was still booming as he climbed off the bed and went into the bathroom and started the shower. He turned it to cold and jumped in, aiming it as his swollen parts. The pain subsided and, when he looked down, it appeared that the bleeding had stopped, so he stood there for a minute more before drying himself off and going back into the bedroom.

'I can't believe you did that!' he shouted at Bethany.

It was then that Stevie realised she had not moved since she landed on the floor. He picked her up and shook her to rouse her, but she didn't move. A horrible thought flashed through his mind, but he was aware Bethany had been out of it before this happened and he was hoping that this was the reason she didn't respond. He put her on the bed, gave her a real shake and called her name. There was no movement. He felt for a pulse as he had seen people do on TV but couldn't feel one.

A little bit of him clung to the thought that he hadn't done it correctly, but that small hope slowly washed away with the realisation that she was not breathing.

Bethany was dead.

Stevie shook her again, listened for her breathing and tried for a pulse again. There was no response. He dropped her onto the bed and sat back to try to gather his thoughts.

What should he do? Should he call the police and explain what had happened, that it was an accident? They wouldn't believe him. A middle-aged man in a bedroom with a young girl, and she had accidently fallen and bumped her head? No way.

And if they looked into his previous history, Stevie knew he had a record because of the fire at the nightclub. He hadn't been charged with anything in the end but knew from a friendly detective that he had been a main suspect all the way through the enquiry. Something like this "accident" would be one too many, and they would throw the book at him.

He made himself another coffee, suddenly feeling sober and sick at the same time. He thought through what had happened that evening. No one really knew he and Bethany had been together. They had left the restaurant separately; it had only been a chance meeting at the bus stop that no one else would have seen. In the pub, it was so busy and noisy that even though people had seen them together, no one knew who they were and what their relationship was.

When they had got back to the hotel, nobody was around. There would have been CCTV, but the chances of that catching them was remote. So, no one knew she was here, and no one knew she was with him.

Stevie felt a wave of relief. When Bethany was reported missing, nothing would lead them to him. Only one problem: how to get rid of the body?

He could put her in the boot of his car, take her up to the cliffs at Beachy Head just up the road and throw her over.

Everyone would think it was a suicide, and any injuries that she had would be masked by the tumble down the five-hundred-foot cliff. Stevie knew from his conversations with her that Bethany had had a troubled childhood, so a suicide wouldn't surprise anyone.

But the idea had flaws. A car driving up there in the middle of the night would be spotted. No, he had to get rid of her without using his car, as it was traceable.

He needed to think of a way to move the body. She wasn't big, so it should be easy. He was glad his brain seemed to have cleared, and he made himself another coffee.

He put the *'Do Not Disturb'* sign on the door. That would give him until twelve o'clock to come up with a plan.

CHAPTER TWENTY

A s early morning sun filtered into the room, Stevie showered and prepared himself for the day ahead. He went over and over the plan in his mind to make sure there was no way he would get caught.

He realised that if he could avoid any connection to Bethany, he would get away with it, and his new plan seemed to cover everything. He had tried to think back to all the TV detective programmes he had watched and remember how the suspects had been caught out.

The first thing he needed to do was to go out and buy some equipment. He decided to only use cash, which he always carried, to buy items in different shops where possible, and to avoid the town centre, where the main CCTV cameras were. He knew that detectives would later trawl through footage from those cameras, and if he could try to blend in and not do anything too extreme, nobody would notice him.

Stevie put on a baseball cap and pulled it low, adding a pair of sunglasses over his eyes, again to hide his identity but without making himself look too unusual. He then walked out of the hotel and turned right towards the shops.

The first item he bought in a small corner shop was a roll of decent-quality bin liners. He then went to a hardware shop and bought some black masking tape and a large roll of industrial kitchen towels. His next purchase was from a shop that seemed to sell all kinds of everything, where he bought a pair of rubber gloves and a set of kitchen knives. Not the best quality, he knew, but they would serve him well for what he needed to do.

His final purchases were the ones he was worried about, as he wasn't sure where he could buy what he needed without going into the main Beacon shopping centre, something he wanted to avoid due to CCTV cameras. On the road leading from the seafront to the town centre was a large TJ Hughes store. Stevie knew from the ones he had visited in the past that these were discount stores selling exactly what he wanted. He must have gone before he met Suzie, he mused, as she wouldn't be seen dead in one of those.

Seen dead! Oh my God, he thought, *what have I done?*

Stevie stopped for a few seconds to recover his breath and compose himself. Then he went into the store and down to the basement, where he chose small and medium-sized matching suitcases. After purchasing them, he put the smaller one inside the other and walked off down the street to the Travelodge, pulling the case behind him. In a holiday town it didn't look out of place at all.

Once at the hotel, he went through the foyer, pulling his case. Again, he didn't look out of place, and anyway the receptionist was too busy sorting out a couple of disgruntled customers, who were moaning that they hadn't been able to sleep because of the sound of the seagulls. Stevie desperately wished his current troubles were as trivial as that.

CHAPTER TWENTY-ONE

Crofts woke up before the alarm, feeling refreshed. He'd had a good sleep, unlike when he was on call. Those nights he would often wake several times just to check he hadn't missed a message; the minimal amount of pay he got for being on standby not compensating for the disrupted rest.

However, that wasn't the case last night. A lack of sleep the night before, a long, busy day and a couple of glasses of red had resulted in a deep sleep, setting him up for the day ahead. He jumped up, turned the alarm off so that it didn't wake Debs and headed into the bathroom for a shave and a shower. He then went downstairs, put the kettle on and turned on Radio Two.

He heard footsteps bouncing down the stairs. They were only small, but they were very loud, as Oscar tried to get down as fast as possible.

'Hi, Dad. What's for breakfast?' he asked. Crofts smiled; it felt like Oscar was at an age where he ate for England.

'Well, sir, there's a choice of Coco Pops, Weetabix or toast this morning,' answered Crofts in his best waiter's voice.

'I'll have the Weetabix then, please!' Oscar replied in a similar vein.

Crofts got his breakfast ready, and they sat down to eat and discuss their favourite subject: football.

'Do you think Brighton will ever get into the Champions League?' Oscar asked.

'Maybe one day,' Crofts replied, knowing it was unlikely.

'So, there's no chance of us buying the next Messi or Ronaldo is there?'

That was an easy one.

'No way, José,' he replied.

'Don't say that to me. It reminds me of Mourinho!' Oscar joked.

Crofts laughed, just as Deborah came in for her breakfast. The three of them chatted about the weekend ahead. Oscar was looking forward to it too, as the BBQ just happened to be at one of his friends' houses, meaning everybody would have a great time.

Crofts then said his goodbyes, receiving a big kiss from both, before jumping on his bike and heading to the office, U2 singing about 'Sunday Bloody Sunday' as he rode.

Arriving at the patrol centre, he swiped his card at the front gate, and it swung open for him. He parked his bike in the racks and walked into the building. As quite often happened, Crofts was the first in the office, except of course for Estella, the cleaner who started at around five. She had just finished the actual SOCO office and it smelt slightly of polish – much better than some of the smells that wafted out of that room.

Crofts went to the seniors' area, a small partitioned-off part of the office and started up his computer. Once he'd booked on, he checked who was on duty and then gathered the cups and headed round to the tea point to make drinks for the rest of his staff.

He was carrying a trayful of teas and coffees back round to the office as the others started turning up. Crofts told Leighton and Hannah to let the control room know that the two of them would be working back at the scene with him today. He spotted the disappointed looks from one or two of the others.

All SOCOs loved working on major jobs. It got them away from the normal routine of stolen cars and burglaries. It always made Crofts laugh that his staff preferred to be at a grotty, smelly scene all day rather than driving around visiting nice houses. That was the nature of the SOCO.

He grabbed his blue investigator's notebook and his cup of tea and went upstairs to the major incident briefing room. Early morning briefings usually meant a full room, as everyone involved in the investigation would come together to give an update on what had happened the day before and overnight. There would have been a briefing the evening before, but Crofts had been busy at the PM, so this was his first chance to give an update.

Tom Mead, as SIO, explained the job for the benefit of anyone just joining the team and then asked everyone to introduce themselves. As Crofts expected, the first couple of people were detectives from the major crime team. The analysts and typists who worked in the incident room, inputting all the information onto the HOLMES crime management computer system, introduced themselves next, followed by the sergeant in charge of the house-to-house investigation team, and the sergeant in charge of the search team. Crofts was next, and then an inspector from the Hastings area, who would be organising the response to the crime, and would be gauging the impact on the local community. There was also a press liaison. Their role was to help let the public know what was going on, although in most cases they tried to keep a lid on what information was given out to avoid hampering the investigation. The investigation team might also need help from the public and may need to appeal for witnesses.

Once the introductions had finished, Mead gave an update on the investigations so far, explaining the scene, the victim, the suspects and the post-mortem. He then asked for an update from all parties in the room. Two of the detectives had interviewed a couple of the individuals from the squat, but neither had seen nor heard anything suspicious on the night in question. This did bring into question their state of mind at the time, and if, indeed, anyone would have noticed anything anyway.

It appeared that another Lithuanian, called Belikas, was the last person who had been seen with the victim, roughly an hour before the phone call to police. It came as no surprise to anyone that he had since disappeared. The main priority of the investigation would be to trace him and arrest him. All local units, uniform, PCSOs and detectives would be given his photo and information. The sooner he was arrested, the better.

Crofts gave his update from the scene and the PM, and then all the other officers gave theirs. Mead then provided some actions for the detectives to carry out and arranged a briefing for six o'clock that evening, and everyone left, except Crofts. He and Mead needed to discuss how the investigation would be approached and to make a decision on how thorough the examination at the scene would need to be. For this particular job it was an easy conversation, unlike some scenes, where the SIO's requests hadn't gone down too well with the senior SOCO.

Crofts started, 'I'm sure you'll agree we don't need to carry out a full forensic examination of the whole building in this instance.'

'It's just a waste of everyone's time,' Mead agreed, 'and isn't going to help prove the crime anyway.'

Crofts liked the sound of that. 'I'm happy to carry out a full forensic search in the room that the body was found, as it appears to be the only area in question. We can take DNA swabs from all areas and from items of social interaction, and any further forensic samples needed, and then fingerprint the room as well, if that suits you?'

'Sounds good,' replied Mead. 'That'll mean that Trevor and his search team can start looking through the rest of the building whilst you're working away.'

'Great. I'll go and update the forensic strategy and send you a copy, and we'll start at the scene as soon as we can. I'll add the samples and actions that are needed for when we arrest the suspect.'

Crofts went back down to his office and called the two SOCOs over to give them an update on the briefing. He then explained what needed to be done at the scene.

'So, grab a quick cuppa and then head on over there. I'll just complete the strategy and then I'll catch you up. By the way, I don't take sugar in my tea!'

Leighton rolled his eyes and wandered off to the tea point with a tray full of mugs. As usual in the office, if you offered to make one person a drink, you ended up making one for everyone.

Crofts set about composing the forensic strategy, a job that came easily to him, as he often wrote several of them in a day, although the one required for a murder was much more detailed. It also had to be correct and precise, since the outcome of any investigation depended on how that strategy was set and how it was followed. Any later reviews of the investigation would also comment on the decisions made, whether good or bad.

If there was ever an investigation failure, which was rare, the two things that were criticised the most were the SIO's policy book and the forensic strategy. Crofts was proud of the fact that none of his strategies had ever been brought into question.

CHAPTER TWENTY-TWO

At the Foyer, Ronnie Jackson was busying himself with the many jobs of a duty manager. The main thing was that he didn't have to deal with residents at this hour. Most wouldn't surface for some time yet.

He knew Bethany would be coming downstairs soon, and he looked forward to seeing her. She was quirky, but there was something endearing about her. He loved the way he could embarrass her, something none of the other girls staying there would allow. In fact, Ronnie knew that most of the other girls didn't like him, and they made it obvious.

He had once overheard one of them saying that he was 'creepy and a perv', which upset him. He was only trying to be friendly. He enjoyed this job; it paid well and suited him. It wasn't what he had wanted to do on leaving school, as he'd wanted to be a teacher.

Having gone to the local polytechnic, he'd got good enough grades to go to what was then called teacher training college. Everything had gone well on the course until he went for a placement at a junior school. The problem was that he had started to become attracted to the young children. He didn't know why, as he hadn't felt that way before, but they were so lovely. And they had looked up to him as their teacher, which had made him feel even more wanted.

He knew he could never show his feelings whilst at work, but when he got home in the evenings he would fantasise about them. This was the eighties and before the internet, so there was no way of contacting any like-minded individuals. Ronnie knew there must be other people like him, but it wasn't a question he could ask anyone, especially with his job.

One day, he and a couple of mates had gone up to London for a day out. After a few drinks the group went to Soho for a bit of entertainment. First stop was a peep show. The men each entered a small booth, which stank of fish and had soiled tissues on the floor. They inserted a pound coin into a slot, the viewing window opened and a half-naked girl began writhing around on a pedestal in front of them. Just as it looked like she was going to complete the striptease, the money ran out. Another coin was needed before the whole charade continued.

Ronnie noticed that you could see the other viewers' faces all around the room in different stages of ecstasy – or not, depending on what they thought of the show. It didn't do anything for him, but he'd stayed for a few minutes without putting any money in, then met up with his mates. Everyone else had enjoyed the show, and Ronnie joined in with the banter.

They decided to try one of the many clubs along the way. They knocked on the door of one of them, which was opened by a very attractive young lady who had wrapped a curtain around her to hide her nakedness from the outside world.

'Hi, guys, what do you want?' she asked, looking them up and down like she'd already decided that they weren't the type of clients the club wanted.

'We'd like to come in for a drink,' replied Bob, one of the lads.

'I had better warn you it's about twenty pounds a drink in here. Not sure that's what you want?' she said in a forced friendly voice. The club's bosses probably didn't want four drunken twenty-somethings in the club nursing one drink when she could attract wealthy gentlemen who were willing to spend a fortune for a little attention.

'Blimey, that's a bit steep. I think we'll go elsewhere,' replied Bob.

'No problem,' the girl said, and then she gave them a seductive wink, which almost made Bob ejaculate there and then.

'Oh gosh,' was all he could say. 'Let's find somewhere else.'

So, having realised Soho wasn't what they expected it to be, the group ended up in a bookshop that sold many and varied magazines. There were magazines of every different type of fetish and sexual kink you could imagine.

Each of them found something unusual to show to each other – rubber gear, bondage and S&M. While this merriment was going on, Ronnie spotted something in a corner of the room that caught his eye. It was a group of magazines with naked children on the front, and he almost ran over to open one but realised he couldn't with the others around.

Everyone bought a couple of magazines each and then they headed for the next pub. Ronnie was desperate to go back to the shop, the images from the front covers imprinted on his mind. If the cover photos were doing that to him, he wondered what the photos inside would be like. The rest of the evening was a blur as more drinks were consumed.

Ronnie knew he wouldn't be able to get to the shop that day, but the following day he went back on a train on his own. He went straight to the shop and bought five different magazines. Once home, he spent the rest of that day feasting his eyes on them. There were also contact numbers for like-minded people. He eventually plucked up the courage to call one of the numbers and was introduced to the large, secret world of the paedophile.

He soon became a player in this world, meeting others and even engaging in sexual acts with children. This, however, did affect his career as a teacher.

There had been several complaints about him from parents, who had seen how he interacted with their children and hadn't liked it. He was interviewed by a couple of different headteachers, but no action was ever taken, and he was only ever told to be mindful of his actions around the children. In one case he was reported to the police and brought in for questioning, but nothing was ever proven. In fact, nothing had actually taken place; it was just the way Ronnie was perceived.

He wasn't stupid. He realised that if he was going to stay undiscovered in the paedophile world, working around children, as lovely as it was, would have to stop. So he had moved over to the field of social care, firstly helping people with mental health issues, and then going on to work with younger people in general.

With the onset of the internet, his hidden world became so much easier to access. Once the police began to realise what was going on and started investigating that world, the paedophiles upped their game, so that now they were always one step ahead of the authorities.

Ronnie had learnt over the years that within his network of friends there were some very high-ranking officials from all walks of life, and everyone would look after each other when needed. So now he was here. The internet made sure it was easy for him to satisfy his desires, and he worked with an age group that he didn't usually fancy. That was until Bethany turned up. She was tiny, almost the size of a ten-year-old, and with her exotic make-up she fulfilled two of his favourite fantasies. It was just a matter of waiting for the right moment, and over the years he had learnt to wait.

CHAPTER TWENTY-THREE

Stevie was putting his plan into motion. First, he cut up a few of the bin liners and stuck them together on the floor, making a large groundsheet. He then lined both cases with some of the black bags. Then he put the body into the bath, hoping all the blood would drain down into it, meaning he could wash it away easily afterwards. Next, he put on the Marigold gloves, knowing that these would keep him protected from the body fluids and prevent him from leaving fingerprints.

Now was the moment he was dreading. He was going to have to cut Bethany's arms, head and legs off so that he could distribute the parts into the two suitcases. He tried not to look at her face, hoping to dehumanise the whole process, but her eyes stared back at him. He had originally tried to close them, as he had seen done in films, but it hadn't worked. So he had to carry on with them open, which was unsettling.

Stevie had gone over all the options time and time again, and this still seemed the only one that would work. All he had to do was get rid of the body, and then he would be able to get on with his life, as there was no connection between him and her.

He took her mobile phone, removed the battery and the

SIM card and placed them into a separate TJ Hughes carrier bag. Stevie then took the largest knife and cut through the shoulder. It was quite easy, and the knife glided through the muscle. It only needed one extra chop around the cartilage area joining the arm to the shoulder and the first arm was free. Stevie carefully made sure all the blood drained out before wrapping it in another bin liner, securing it with tape and laying it in the suitcase. He then moved on to the other arm and repeated the process.

Next it was a leg. This proved to be much tougher and needed a lot more pressure on the hip bone, but the kitchen knives were an easy match for the tough sinew, and he cut through it without too much trouble. He let the blood drain out and then continued with the second leg. Once that was finished, he approached the neck area so that he could sever the head off.

This really was tough work, and he could feel himself sweating with exertion. He ended up almost having to saw through the last part of the spinal column, but finally the head was free. Once drained, Stevie wrapped it in another bin liner, taped it up and then put it in with the limbs in three more bin liners, each individually taped.

Eventually everything was secured. He filled the final gaps in the suitcase with the remaining bin liners. By the time he had done that, the blood had finished draining out of the torso, so Stevie then wrapped that in four individually taped bin liners and also inserted the groundsheet he had made into the second case, all the time making sure there was no blood transferred to the outside of the cases.

Happy that all of it was clean, Stevie put his clothing into another bin liner, taped it up and put it into the TJ Hughes bag to carry separately. He checked his watch; it was only eleven. He still had an hour before he needed to check out, so there was not too much of a rush. He turned on the shower and let it run for a while before pouring plenty of shower gel into the bath itself and the sink, and then using some kitchen towel to wipe down all areas that could potentially have traces of blood. He then flushed all the paper rubbish down the toilet. He knew that the room would be cleaned by the maids later that day, so this was just an extra wash.

Finally, Stevie stood in the shower, making plenty of lather with the gel, and scrubbed himself from head to toe. Happy that he was clean, he towelled himself dry and put on a fresh set of clothes. He had decided not to wear a suit like normal and instead pulled on jeans and a plain T-shirt, as he had more work to do. He added his baseball cap and glasses and walked out of the room, checking that nothing looked out of keeping with a guest who had stayed for the night.

The suitcases didn't seem too heavy. He had guessed that splitting the body between the two cases would mean that both weighed something similar to a normal holiday suitcase, and he was right. He walked through the foyer and dropped his key in the hole in the desk as required. The receptionist was busy on the phone, so again he went unnoticed.

Stevie walked around the corner to where his car was parked and dropped his overnight bag in the boot. He wasn't going to use that for the next part of his plan but would need it later. He started walking towards the railway station; again he didn't look out of place pulling two suitcases along, as others were doing the same around him.

His first stroke of luck came just around the corner as he turned and noticed a refuse lorry heading along the street towards him, the binmen walking ahead and dragging the bins from each gateway. Stevie quickly opened one of the bins next to where he stood and threw the carrier bag containing his clothes and the mobile phone parts into it. He then walked another few yards and stopped to look at his phone. It was then that he remembered he needed to turn it off, since he didn't want to be traced for the next part of his journey. He waited agonisingly for the bin lorry to reach him. The two binmen pulling the bins out were chatting to each other about football and not paying attention to anything around them.

Stevie almost stopped breathing as he watched the bin containing his clothes being hooked onto the back of the truck and automatically lifted and tipped up. He saw the lorry's internal metal wall move forward to crush the contents of the bins together. Surely all of his clothes were now mashed with all of the other refuse so that they would never be found.

Stevie sighed in relief and carried on walking towards the station. In the ticket office, he asked for a cheap day return to London and paid cash. He then bought a coffee and a savoury pastry and got on the train.

Having found an area for his suitcases, he sat down with his food and drink to await the journey.

It only takes an hour and a half to get to London from Eastbourne, but it seemed a lot longer to Stevie. The train was quiet to start with, but at each stop more people got on until it reached East Croydon, where it was so full that people were standing. He did think about the possibility that someone would notice something untoward about the suitcases and decided that if anyone did, he would just get off at the next stop, pretending the cases weren't his. As he kept on telling himself, there was no way to connect him and Bethany anyway.

Nobody even noticed the cases. Everyone was too busy looking at phones, iPads or newspapers. When the train finally arrived at Victoria, everyone rushed to get off. Stevie waited until there was room and then slowly lifted the cases down and walked off along the platform with them.

Once through the ticket barrier, he made his way straight to the left luggage area. It was fairly busy when he got there. The guy who served him was Eastern European and didn't speak English too well but was happy to take the money Stevie offered and gave him a receipt. It was paid for by the day, and so Stevie paid for seven days. Hopefully that would be enough time.

He then went back to the platform and caught the train back to Eastbourne. He couldn't believe how simple it had all been. The whole procedure had gone nice and easy, and Stevie was sure no one would be able to connect him to Bethany at any stage.

He almost fell asleep once the train had gathered speed but made sure he kept himself awake for the journey. He still had one more task to fulfil. On arrival in Eastbourne, he turned his phone back on and walked to his car. He drove out of Eastbourne in an easterly direction, heading towards Ashford, which was where he was due to attend a meeting the following morning.

On the outskirts of the town, he pulled into a Premier Inn and checked in. He had already booked it over the weekend when planning his week, so as far as anyone knew he was on track for his work schedule.

CHAPTER TWENTY-FOUR

Sandy thought it was strange Bethany was late, as she'd never been before. She decided she would give it half an hour in case the bus was late and busied herself with organising the new menus. Forty minutes later, when Bethany had still not arrived, she went to double-check the staff rotas to make sure it was one of Bethany's working days. Of course it was. And the last thing Bethany had said the night before was that she would see her in the morning.

She went into the kitchen and asked her husband, Malcolm, and then Eddy whether either of them had seen her, or whether Bethany had mentioned anything about not coming in.

Malcolm laughed and said, 'That's very unlikely. I don't think I've ever had a full conservation with her in all the time she's worked for us!'

Eddy chipped in with a 'Me neither!'

Sandy walked out into the restaurant, where two other waitresses were setting up tables, and asked the same question. She could tell from the glances between them that Bethany wasn't exactly their best friend, but then that was because she kept herself to herself.

Sandy texted Bethany to see if there was a problem, and when there was no reply, she tried ringing, but it only went to voicemail. She left a message but was still worried; she thought it was odd and so out of character.

She decided to ring the Foyer to see if Bethany was there, and if not, to leave her a message. Ronnie Jackson answered. Sandy introduced herself and explained her concerns.

Ronnie replied, 'I must admit, I do normally see her when she leaves in the morning, and I didn't this morning, but that might have been because I had to go and speak to a couple of coppers. They turned up this morning about an alleged assault on one of our guests in a nightclub, so I wasn't watching all of the time.'

Sandy repeated that it was very unusual, so Ronnie said he would go up to Bethany's room and knock on the door, if Sandy could hold on. Sandy agreed.

She heard his footsteps returning to the phone.

'No reply,' he said. 'But I've stuck a note under her door to contact me or you when she gets back.'

'Are you able to use a skeleton key to enter the room to check she's okay?' Sandy asked.

'I'm afraid not. It's more than my job's worth. It's all to do with the residents' privacy. The only time I can do that is if someone is missing for more than twenty-four hours. I'll log our conversation in the occurrence book, and if we haven't heard from her by tomorrow morning I can look then.'

'Oh all right,' said Sandy, a little dejected.

'I know it sounds a bit harsh, but unfortunately in places like this we do get a lot of residents going missing, and the police aren't interested anyway, due to our clientele's previous history in a lot of cases. They won't get involved until then either.'

Sandy said she understood and would call him the next day if she heard nothing.

She put down the phone and thought about whether to bring another waitress on at short notice. Most of the girls were local and needed the money, so there never a problem calling them. It wouldn't be overly busy, according to the reservations so far, but Bethany was such a good worker that she decided she would need someone in to cover for her. She scrolled through the list of names on her phone before calling Ellie, who sounded pleased to come in.

CHAPTER TWENTY-FIVE

Crofts had spent about an hour preparing the forensic strategy, before he emailed it to Tom Mead to approve. Whilst waiting for the reply, he checked through his many emails.

Crofts remembered the days before computers. His boss at the time would come into work after a couple of days off to find about three Post-it notes with messages on his desk. Nowadays, when he had two days off, he would sometimes return to find eighty emails, most of which he didn't need to read. In a lot of cases, his staff and others would copy him in to messages to make him aware of what was going on and to cover themselves. It meant that he didn't have to do anything with these messages except save them, but it all took time, and hidden in that list were emails that did need actioning.

He scanned through to make sure there wasn't anything too important and then checked the shared library where the leave requests were held. Crofts had always had the opinion that giving his staff time off when needed was one of the most important parts of his role as a supervisor. The job expected them to work extended hours at the drop of a hat at certain times, and all of them did. Crofts maintained that the staff then deserved time off when they needed it. There were guidelines on how many staff had to be on duty at any time, but if that was covered, he would always try to get the requests cleared as soon as possible.

He had just finished when the reply from the SIO popped up in his inbox. The simple message told him that Mead was happy with the strategy and asked that he be kept updated with any findings. Crofts replied in the affirmative and then gathered his equipment together and walked out to his car and headed back on the road to Hastings.

As he drove, he wondered how many times he had been along this road over the years. Too many to count, since Hastings was where the majority of their work was found. He put on Radio Two and listened to *PopMaster* with Ken Bruce. As usual, he only got about three of the answers right from both of the contestants' questions. He had always fancied going on the quiz but was worried he wouldn't be able to answer any questions, and he knew how embarrassing that would be.

He stopped at a café on the approach road to Hastings and bought three coffees to go. Once outside the scene, he told the guard to shout to Hannah and Leighton to tell them he was there. The two of them appeared a minute later, taking their gloves, masks and shoe covers off once they left the building. Crofts motioned them over to the search team vehicle so the three of them could sit in there for a drink and a chat.

It was always awkward finding a place to eat and have a briefing at scenes, as you had to be out of the public eye; firstly, so no one overheard any conversations, and, secondly, to stop people from seeing you having a drink or meal break. For some reason, certain members of the public got really upset when police, SOCOs and any other emergency service personnel stopped for refreshments. There were always comments such as

'We pay your wages' and 'You haven't got time to eat, you should be working' thrown at them. It annoyed Crofts. If there were four plumbers having breakfast in a café, no one would take any notice, but if there were uniformed services, some people couldn't wait to report it.

Crofts asked them how they were getting on, and they gave him a quick update. He could sense from Leighton's response that he wasn't happy about something, so he asked him what the problem was.

'It all seems a waste of our time. We're doing all of this work, and it won't go anywhere. No one will ever get done for murder in this sort of job. Even if we find fingerprints or DNA on the syringe, it won't prove who killed him.'

'I know, I know,' said Crofts. 'But you know as well as anyone that this is the job. We've got to be as thorough as possible. What happens afterwards in court or anywhere else is out of our hands.'

Leighton smiled. 'I know, but sometimes on jobs like this it feels that we are just recovering it all for the sake of it.'

'I know it does, but as long as we approach every scene as we do, we can always say we have done our job properly, and that's what matters.'

Leighton rolled his eyes in mock disgust. 'Sometimes you can be such a Sussex Police spokesman!'

Crofts grinned. 'That's why I'm a supervisor. I have to make sure you non-believers comply!'

All three of them laughed. It wasn't the first time that this type of discussion had taken place. Sometimes the staff didn't see the bigger picture, and it was up to Crofts and his fellow seniors to make sure everyone understood what their actions could lead to. He actually agreed with what Leighton had said and had even made that point to detective inspectors in the past, but due to criticism about the investigation of a drugs-related death the previous year, force policy had been changed to ensure that these types of deaths were treated as murder until proven otherwise. It made things easier for Crofts, as it meant that everyone knew what they were doing at each scene.

They finished their coffees, put on their PPE and went back into the scene. It was quite noisy in the building today, as the search teams were busy going over each flat from top to bottom. The teams had their own strategy, which listed the items for them to recover. The state of the rooms meant plenty of expletives could be heard, as the officers found items they wouldn't find in their own homes, such as used needles and faeces. No matter how experienced the searchers were, a squat such as this would yield plenty of unusual items that most people wouldn't believe. The exclamations and coarse language made Crofts smile. It was a good job the public couldn't hear what was going on. Their perception of the police would certainly change.

He helped the other two SOCOs swab and fingerprint every single area of the room the body had been found in. It was a slow process again, as most of their work was, but they eventually finished at seven in the evening.

After helping to take the two hundred exhibits out to Hannah's van, Crofts called Tom Mead to tell him that everything requested on the strategy had been recovered.

'Thanks for that,' Mead said. 'I think the search teams are finished too. I'll leave the scene guard on until we get some results from the lab with regards to fingerprints and DNA. Did you say we should have some tomorrow?'

'Hopefully,' replied Crofts, making a mental note to give them a ring first thing to make sure.

Mead gave him an update of what had happened at the briefing, which wasn't much at this stage, and Crofts and his team headed back to the office.

CHAPTER TWENTY-SIX

Linas Belikas had realised there was something wrong as soon as he had come around from the hit that he and Jonny had taken together. In his drug-fuddled mind, he couldn't work it out at first, as he seemed to have been out for some time, and he didn't feel too good. He had looked over at Jonny, his best friend on the streets, and saw him staring wide-eyed whilst lying flat on his back. He had called his name and then shaken Jonny, but with no response. It slowly dawned on him that Jonny was dead.

He had seen dead people before. In fact, it was almost an occupational hazard in his world. He knew there was nothing he could do, so he had left as soon as he possibly could, making sure nobody saw him go. It wasn't hard; it seemed everyone in the building was out of it. It did cross his addled mind that maybe there was a problem with the batch of drugs that they had taken, but there was nothing he could do about that either.

He wandered down the street until he found a telephone kiosk, then called the police and gave the details. He half hoped someone might be able to bring Jonny round. Maybe the paramedics could give him an antidote or something. He suspected that it wouldn't be possible, and that it was probably the end of his best mate Jonny.

Tears welled in his eyes as the reality set in, but it was outweighed by the knowledge that he had to get away from the kiosk and, in fact, away from the area, as the police would be calling. They would pick on him and the others in the squat and try to nail poor Jonny's death on them.

With tears rolling down his face, he started jogging towards the seafront. It wasn't really a jog, with his damaged body it was more of a scuffle. Once he got to the seafront, Linas calmed down. He knew plenty of others sleeping along there in different spaces, so he felt at home.

He found an area at the back of the amusement park, underneath a shed used as a ticket office. He curled up, and then the tears returned in large sobs. He cried for his friend and he cried for his life. He fell asleep crying, something he hadn't done for many years.

Linas slept a deep sleep, and when he awoke he guessed it was mid-morning. Time didn't matter to him, but the amount of traffic on the seafront and the number of people walking around confirmed that he was right. He lay down and thought of the evening's events, and everything slowly returned to him.

He wasn't sure what to do next, but he needed water and a hit of something to bring him to life. Crawling out from under the cabin, he heard a scream and saw a young girl aged about four pointing at him and crying. He hadn't meant to scare her, but there was nothing he could do about it. The girl's mother, maybe nineteen and either pregnant or overweight, was screaming at him as well.

'Get away from my kiddie, you fucking low life!'

Linas would normally have argued back, but this time he didn't bother. He just turned and ran towards the Rock-a-Nore area at the end of the seafront, where he knew some of his fellow drifters would be.

Across the road, there were two funicular railways, which took people up the cliffs. Behind the West Hill railway was an area where addicts would meet to jack up out of public view. As soon as Linas got in through the gap in the fence, he saw two men helping each other find veins to inject themselves. They looked much like him, scruffily dressed, skinny and with a haunted look in their eyes. Linas knew both on nodding terms. They were English, but he had never had a problem with them so felt safe.

'Any chance of a quick hit? I'm desperate,' Linas pleaded.

'What you got for it?' asked the younger of the two, who Linas guessed was only about twenty-five.

'Nothing at the moment, but I can get you anything you want later. I just need something right now.'

He saw them glance at each other and make a decision.

'Okay then, mate,' said the taller of the two. 'But you better get back here this afternoon with some booze. Not just crap cider. We want the good vodka, and you Polish know where to get it.'

Linas wasn't bothered about the fact that they had got his nationality wrong, and he was pleased it was only vodka they wanted, as he could get that easily.

'I'm Robbie and this is Spike.'

'Linas,' he replied, and they bumped fists.

Robbie handed Linas a syringe. He didn't ask what was in it. It didn't matter. All he needed was to feel that fluid coursing through his veins. The needle slipped easily into one of the many track marks in his left arm, and he pushed the plunger in slowly, releasing the mixture into his body, feeling it travel through him straight away. He dropped the empty syringe on the ground, where it landed next to many others, then sat down with his back against the wall, closed his eyes and let the sensation spread through his body. Colours danced across his view, and he drifted into the wondrous feeling that drugs gave him, into a world that he couldn't describe to non-users.

Linas was out of it for some time. He didn't know how long, but when he came back round, he found himself with Robbie and Spike, who were in their own drug-induced world, and slowly coming around themselves.

'Thanks, guys. That feels much better,' Linas slurred to them.

'Don't forget some vodka,' Robbie replied. 'If you can get us plenty, you might even get another hit off us.'

Linas replied with a grin that showed how few teeth he had left.

'Before dark tonight!' Spike added.

'No problem,' called Linas as he climbed through the hole in the fence and back out towards the town centre.

Linas walked to the local shops. In one of the side streets, he found a Bargain Booze store. The woman behind the counter was busy with a customer who was collecting a parcel, scanning and sticking labels. He grabbed a bottle of Smirnoff and tucked it under his jacket. It wasn't his vodka of choice, but he knew the two English boys would like it. He then just walked brazenly out of the shop.

The pregnant Indian woman behind the counter shouted out to him, but he just kept walking with his head down. It didn't worry her. She guessed that he had stolen something, and as it would have been recorded on CCTV, they could download the images and contact the police. It was easier than confrontation with these types of people.

Linas was back with Robbie and Spike within an hour, together with his vodka. He was welcomed with open arms once they spotted the bottle. It appeared that this was going to be a good friendship on both sides. They cracked open the vodka and mixed it with some white cider and then guzzled it for the rest of the day. They bonded by telling stories about their lives, before taking another hit, which made them all slip into a better world for the evening, and then they slept fitfully through the night.

CHAPTER TWENTY-SEVEN

L uke Smith had been walking the streets for three months now as a Police Community Support Officer – or PCSO, as they were known.

Luke had wanted to join the police for as long as he could remember. He'd joined the cadets as soon as he was able, aged thirteen, and loved wearing the uniform and learning about all the aspects of policing. It was so much more interesting than school. Every Wednesday night they paraded at the patrol centre in Eastbourne. There would be an inspection, then a drill, before various training scenarios were acted out. Sometimes there were guest speakers, which he loved. Every aspect of police work was covered, and he enjoyed all parts of it. At weekends, there was sometimes the chance to help out at local events, mainly as a traffic guide at the car parks or answering questions from the public, but he felt like he was doing real police work.

When he left school, Luke went to East Sussex College in the town, where he joined the public services course. He really enjoyed it. It involved plenty of physical exercise, he learnt about all aspects of the armed and emergency services, and the course was run by three ex-cops. It also included several weekends away – map-reading and yomping across Dartmoor, and then at Capel Curig, in Wales. Luke lapped it up and finished with a distinction.

The instructors had recommended that Luke should experience a bit of life away from the police before joining, but he couldn't wait. As soon as he'd seen the advert for more PCSOs, he knew that it was the way forward. He would work for a couple of years in that role before joining as a regular. He'd passed the interview stages with ease and started with an intake of twenty, of which he was easily the youngest. It didn't bother him at all. His keenness was infectious, and the others on the course loved him. It was no surprise to any of them when he won the Best Recruit trophy.

Luke was stationed in Hastings, which was his choice, as he didn't want to work in his home town, as many others had recommended he shouldn't. From day one he got stuck in, firstly by getting to know as many people in the station as possible (although his forward manner did ruffle some feathers amongst the older officers). Out on the streets he also got to know as many of the locals on his patch as he could.

He was based in the town centre, so there were plenty to meet. From shopkeepers to business owners, taxi drivers, schoolteachers, children and even street drinkers, Luke talked to them all and in his first three months became a well-known figure in the local community.

He was on a late shift today, which had started at three, and after he attended the briefing, he was given a list of jobs and left on his patrol. His first call was to see Mr Patel, the owner of Bargain Booze, who had reported a shoplifter caught on camera.

Luke walked the mile from the nick down to the town centre, and once there made slow progress through the town, stopping every other minute to chat to various people who waved to him or said hello. He loved this part of his job, face-to-face conversations with members of the public, and it was something they liked as well. Especially the older generation as one of their biggest complaints about the modern police force was that the officers didn't have time to talk to them, unlike the coppers from their youth.

Eventually he got to Bargain Booze. The owner welcomed him in again. Luke was called there at least once a week. They went through to the back of the shop, past his pregnant wife, who smiled at Luke, and to the office. The screen in the corner had ten different cameras running. Mr Patel entered a few numbers on the keyboard, and the footage from the previous day was up and running. Luke watched closely as the camera showed the suspect walk in, shamelessly grab a bottle of vodka and walk straight out again. No doubt there had been an offence committed; he now just needed a close-up of the suspect's face. As Mr Patel changed the view to a different camera angle, Luke paled. He realised he had seen the suspect very recently – at the briefing at the beginning of his shift. The man was currently wanted for murder.

'Are you okay?' Mr Patel asked, looking concerned.

'Yes, I'm fine,' Luke replied. 'Just a little hot today. I don't actually know this man, but I have seen him on our local briefing pages, so he must be a prolific offender. If you can download the images from the offence and the close-ups of him, I'll get them back to the station. Once they've been circulated to all patrol officers, I'm sure we'll catch him soon.'

Mr Patel was already burning it all onto a disc. 'Thank you so much for your help and your prompt actions. I hope you catch him soon, and yes, I am happy to go to court!' he said. He was an old hand at these procedures, unfortunately dealing with shoplifting was one of the many pitfalls of running a convenience store.

Luke went outside the shop and called his supervisor to ask for a lift back to the station as soon as possible.

'What's the problem?'

'I'll tell you when I get back, but it is priority, and it's to do with Op Dundee.'

The supervisor, Michael Jones, knew Luke was a little overkeen in some ways, but he also knew he was turning out to be a very good officer and had never asked for a lift back to the station before so guessed it was important. In fact, he thought it was so important that he jumped into the car himself and sped off to pick Luke up.

He was there within minutes.

'What you got then, Luke?' he asked.

'The suspect from Op Dundee. I think I've got him on CCTV shoplifting a bottle of vodka at Bargain Booze yesterday evening,' said Luke quickly, whilst climbing into the car.

'Bloody well done, matey. Good bit of work. The enquiry team will be pleased with that. It means he's still in the area. Let's get up there as soon as possible,' Jones said as he drove the car back up towards the nick. 'By the way, you know that if it is him and if he gets caught, you'll have to buy the cakes? No blue-and-white-striped rubbish. Proper cream cakes.'

'I'm not sure how these cake fines work,' replied Luke. 'You get them when you do something wrong, and now you're saying that I have to buy some when I do something good too?'

The older man laughed. 'You'll get the hang of it one day.'

The supervisor had radioed ahead to let the incident room know there was something for them, so that by the time Luke arrived, all ten people in the room had stopped talking and awaited his findings. Luke felt himself blush but went straight into an update on what had happened at Bargain Booze. Kevin Bates, the room supervisor, was a wily detective sergeant in his late forties, tall and well-built with a shaven head. He played the footage, and the other analysts and detectives watched. Everyone agreed it was their suspect. Luke got plenty of slaps on the back and felt so proud of himself.

Bates then addressed the members of the enquiry team. 'Right, we now know Belikas did not leave Hastings immediately after the body was found and was still here a day later. I want all CCTV from that area checked to see if we can find his route to Bargain Booze and away from it. We can then maybe find out where he is holed up.'

There were murmurs of approval as everyone got to work.

The detective turned to Luke. 'Well done, young man. A good bit of police work. What was your name again?'

Luke blushed once more as he tried to steady his voice enough to reply with his name.

'Well, young Luke, you keep this up. We always need a good lead in any job, and you've just provided us with one.'

Luke turned and walked out of the incident room. He had never been so pleased with himself.

CHAPTER TWENTY-EIGHT

Stevie awoke with a start. For a split second he thought he was back in the Travelodge in Eastbourne again. The panic that gripped his stomach as these thoughts went through his mind was soon overtaken by the knowledge of what had actually happened the day before, and he felt sick. He went into the bathroom and retched in the toilet bowl. All that came up was pungent yellow bile, as he hadn't eaten since Monday evening . He stared into the bowl and watched the evil-smelling mess moving around, realising what he had done.

It hadn't affected him at all the day before.

Stevie had known what his plan was, and once he had started, there wasn't a moment to sit and think about it; he had to keep going. Once he'd arrived back at his car, he had driven almost on autopilot to Ashford and had checked in, showered and gone straight to bed, where he had slept a deep sleep without waking until now. He realised he needed food, and he also needed to carry on as if nothing untoward had happened. His meeting with the regional manager was at eleven, and he knew he had to be on the ball by then.

He had yet another shower, hoping that it would also

remove any last memories of his actions, put on his favourite suit and wandered over to Table Table Restaurant, which was attached to the Premier Inn. They did a good buffet breakfast there, and that was what he needed. Stevie wouldn't normally bother, since he could claim the nine pounds back, and he would buy a cheap sandwich instead, but today was different. He gave his room number to the young girl at the entrance and walked in. He ordered coffee and then went over to the food in the buffet area. He loaded his plate up with one of everything, including black pudding. As he put it on his plate, he remembered it was made from pig's blood, and for a split second he pictured Bethany's blood running into the bath, but he then cleared his mind and sat down for breakfast.

He really was hungry and the plateful was soon gone. He spread some butter and marmalade on the last piece of toast, poured himself a third cup of coffee and then sat back and contemplated what he had done.

He knew he was now a murderer but didn't feel bad about it. He reminded himself again that if he had reported it to the police straight away, he would have been done for murder anyway. A middle-aged man with a young girl dead in his hotel room; he would never have been believed if he'd said it was an accident. In their eyes, he would have been guilty from the minute he made the phone call.

He knew there was no direct connection between him and Bethany. Nobody had seen them in Pevensey Bay, and everyone in the pub had been too drunk to notice. If, after she was reported missing, someone remembered seeing her in the Crown and Anchor, nobody would know who the bloke she had been with was, and he'd just been a guest in a hotel in the town that night. No one would physically connect him to her.

During the trip to Victoria he had worn a baseball cap and sunglasses. No one would be able to identify him, and again, there was no chance of anything being traced back to him. Anyway, that was all done now, and he had to get on with his life as if nothing had happened.

The first thing was to get to Pfizer and speak to the regional manager. So Stevie got his things together and made his way there, arriving fifteen minutes before his appointment. He checked in with the receptionist and sat back and waited.

Jon Thackery was walking towards him within a minute, hand outstretched, ready to shake.

'Stevie, great to see you're here nice and early. I like it,' he said, shaking Stevie's hand firmly, and smiling when Stevie did the same back.

Jon was roughly Stevie's age, with a shaven bald head, fit and well-looking and wearing an expensive suit. They had only met once before, as Jon was originally based in the north region and had only moved down six months before.

'Come on over to my office. We'll get some coffee in there,' he called behind him as he strode towards the lift, Stevie following behind.

Once in the office, having ordered drinks, Jon asked Stevie how things were going. Stevie gave him an update on his last two months' figures, backed up with all of the paperwork he had brought with him. Jon seemed impressed, and Stevie started to relax. He was never sure why he was invited to attend these types of meetings but made sure he was well prepared. If the meeting was to give him bad news, he was always ready for that eventuality.

Stevie then went on to tell him about his meeting on Monday and the size of the contract he had agreed, which would also end up being a national affair. Jon looked even more impressed.

It was now that Stevie decided to go for it. 'There is something I need to talk to you about.'

'What is it?' Jon asked warily.

'I'm not sure if you're aware, but I have young twins.'

'Yes, I remember you telling me.'

'Well, they're harder work than I expected. My wife doesn't cope with them very well, and I was wondering if there was any chance I could transfer to a position that means I'm not on the road all the time?' He noticed Jon's hesitancy, so added, 'I'm happy to move anywhere in the country if that helps.'

Jon was quiet for a moment but smiled. 'I must admit, that was the last thing I expected from you. You've always said that it suited you so well, and you've consistently been the top salesman in the region. However, I can only guess how hard it is with twins. We had our two a couple of years apart, and that was bad enough, so double the trouble must be tough. You do realise there will also be a drop in commission if you become office based, and in your case that would be a substantial amount.'

'Yes, I do, but I've realised that I want to spend more time with them now, and money is secondary. Depending on where and when I'm working, it may make a difference in our plans.'

He had already decided he wasn't going to mention that his plans didn't involve Suzie. That was for him to sort out privately, not something to be discussed in this type of meeting.

'When you said you were happy to move, was there a particular part of the country you would prefer? Us northerners sometimes don't want to leave God's country!'

'Ha ha! I'm not from Yorkshire, if that's where you mean, but I have always had a hankering for the south coast, and as much as I love the north, I think it would be a better lifestyle for the twins.'

Jon had already started looking on his laptop, clicking and typing away. Stevie couldn't tell from his expression what he was up to, or what he was thinking. After what seemed like ages,

Jon clicked one final time with an elaborate flourish and looked at Stevie with earnest.

'Well, I must admit that was a surprise. I had actually called you in to congratulate you on your sales successes yet again, and to tell you what your bonus was going to be. Your request, however, changes things. As you know, there aren't many jobs going that are further up the ladder, but the next one for you would be area manager. What you don't know is that Colin Willis, your area manager, is just about to move back up to the north-east. He requested it a couple of years ago. You know what the Geordies are like. Always want to go home to the Toon!'

Jon laughed at his own joke. Stevie smiled too, as this seemed to be going well.

'Rosie in the north-east has decided to move elsewhere. So that means that Colin can replace her. I was wondering who could fill the gap here, and I think you're the man for it. You would obviously be working under me. Could you cope with that?' he asked with a mock-horror expression on his face.

This changed to a broad smile as Stevie said, 'I would enjoy that, yes.'

'Area managers are based here, but as with most companies now, everyone tends to work from home a lot and you'll only be expected to show your face here once a week, for regional meetings. Day-to-day there may be travel involved, but it will only be to meet up with one of your team, so you can arrange the time to suit you, and it will mean that you can always get home for the little ones' dinner time!'

Stevie couldn't believe his luck. This was exactly what he'd had in mind when he'd first thought of the idea. He also knew that if his plans to move with the twins to Pevensey Bay worked, then that was only about forty miles from Ashford anyway.

'How do I apply for it?' Stevie asked.

'You don't need to,' said Jon with a big smile. 'I'm regional manager, and if I say I want someone on my team, I get it. Anyway, if there was ever a problem, your past sales figures would back up my judgement.'

Jon stood up and stretched his hand out. 'I take it that's a yes?' and before Stevie could answer, his hand was being pumped energetically and Jon was welcoming him to his team.

The next half an hour was spent filling in forms, updating his expenses and generally going over what would be required in his new role. Jon was happy to give him a month to sort out accommodation wherever he decided to move to, the company footing the removal bill. Eventually Stevie managed to get out of the office and back to his car.

He sat and exhaled. What a twenty-four hours he had just had. He decided he was going to head straight home to tell Suzie of his plans. His smile was Cheshire-cat sized.

That old Stevie Johnson magic was back again.

CHAPTER TWENTY-NINE

Sandy guessed Bethany wasn't going to be in this morning. It was so out of character for her to have missed even one day. There must be something wrong. She wished she had tried to get to know Bethany a little more and maybe helped her with any problems.

She realised that the reason she hadn't was Bethany herself. She wouldn't let anyone get that close.

Sandy phoned Ronnie again. He was obviously thinking the same thing at the same time.

'I was expecting your call. We've had no contact either,' Ronnie said. 'I have asked a few people around here if they've seen her, but none of them have. In fact, a lot of them didn't know her too well. She kept herself to herself, which is a shame, as she seems like a nice girl.'

Sandy replied, 'She's the same here at work, and it is a pity, I like her too.'

'What I'll do now,' said Ronnie, 'is use the skeleton key to look in her room. Do you want to stay on the line in case I find anything that may help us work out where she is?'

'Yes, please.' Sandy wondered if Ronnie had had the same thought as her: *Bethany may be in that room.*

As if he had read her mind, he said, 'If there is anything unpleasant when I get into the room, I might not be able to tell you.'

'Oh dear, I hope not,' she replied, but Ronnie said, 'You never know with teenagers.' And then all Sandy could hear was Ronnie's steps up the stairs and along a corridor, until they stopped.

Ronnie inserted the key in the lock, turned it and held his breath.

Sandy could sense his apprehension, even over the phone. She knew he hadn't been joking a moment ago and that he'd found several suicide victims over the years.

There was nothing like that today, however. Bethany definitely wasn't in there.

He told Sandy straight away. She could hear the relief in his voice.

'Looks like everything is in place. Make-up bag and hairdryer on the bed, I would imagine from when she got ready to go out. There's not a lot in here anyway, and not an obvious note or anything like that. It just looks like Bethany has gone out, nothing more.'

'Oh, that's good,' Sandy replied. 'But where do you think she has gone?'

'Not sure, but as I've made this official by going into the room, I'll have to contact the police and report her as a missing person. Do you want me to give them your details as a contact as well, in case she calls when I'm not at work?'

'Yes, please,' said Sandy. 'I feel she's a friend and part of our team, even though she doesn't always want it that way, and I do think that this is so unusual. I can always rely on Bethany.'

Ronnie contacted the police on the 101 non-emergency

number. The operator took all the details down professionally, although Ronnie did notice a slight change in his voice when he said that Bethany was from the Foyer. The police spent a lot of time dealing with problems at the centre, whether assaults or, indeed, missing persons so he imagined the address probably flagged up in their system. He had worked within social services for long enough to know this wasn't going to be a priority.

The operator said he would pass it on and that a local unit would be in touch later that day. Ronnie locked the door to Bethany's room and went back down to the office. He was as puzzled as Sandy. Bethany was one of the less troublesome guests he had to look after, and it was out of character for her. He felt a little guilty about his dirty thoughts about her and just hoped she was safe somewhere.

CHAPTER THIRTY

As excited as Luke Smith had been the night before, he knew the job wasn't finished yet, as Belikas was still at large. Luke also knew that if the suspect was someone who lived on the streets, he would be able to help find him.

He might be young in service, but he was keen and had made it his job to try to connect with the street drinkers, drug users and homeless on his patch. He was aware these people both annoyed and scared the public and if he got to know them, they would be easier for him to deal with. Some of them, however, didn't want contact with anyone, let alone someone in authority. The reasons they were on the streets were often complex, including mental health issues. They were often happier in their own community.

Luke had tried hard and managed to get on the good side of some of them, and so this morning he was out looking for clues within their community. The first two homeless men he had spoken to were locals and had no idea who Jonny or Linas were. In fact, he got a long spiel from them about how the Polish had ruined their lives in Hastings and the easy money they previously got from visitors outside the railway station had all but stopped. The fact that most of these people weren't from Poland but from other countries in the Baltic area didn't matter to them.

Luke managed to get a word in edgeways, finally, to ask where the others might be congregated.

'Anywhere' was the unhelpful answer, followed by further reasons why these types were bad news.

Luke got away eventually and headed down to the seafront, deciding he would just look himself. He had printed off a copy of the suspect's photograph and had it in his pocketbook. The image was also indelibly printed in his memory. As Luke approached the funicular railway, knowing it was an area used for drug taking, he decided to have a look around. He found the hole in the fence.

Pushing his way through, he sensed there were people through there before seeing them. Two comatose forms lay on the floor in the shadows. He knew Robbie and Spike well, as they were always out and about in the town centre begging. He had moved them on plenty of times.

'Wakey-wakey, you two,' he called out.

No doubt seeing the uniform rather than the person, Spike automatically shouted, 'We haven't done anything!'

'I know you haven't. That's not what I want,' replied Luke.

'That's okay then,' came the relieved reply.

Luke waited for them to wake up properly before he continued. 'This is a photo of someone we need to speak to urgently.'

A glance passed between the two men and Luke realised it meant they knew the suspect.

'Not sure,' said Spike.

'Don't lie,' Luke said immediately, and in their muddled minds he could see that they were lost as to what to say next. 'When did you last see him and where?'

'Might've seen him yesterday by the pier,' said Spike.

'I don't believe that. Where is he? If you don't tell me, I'll call the cops and get you arrested for something.'

That changed their demeanour straight away. 'Okay, he was here last night, but we honestly don't know where he is now. He must've gone somewhere this morning. We only woke up when you got here.'

This time Luke believed him. 'Where is he likely to have gone?' They just shrugged.

Luke told them he needed to know, as it was important, and that he would be back later to see them. Just as he got back to the gap in the fence, a skinny denim-clad leg started to climb through. Luke realised it was the suspect as soon as the rest of his body followed. He went to grab Linas, but years of escaping meant that Linas's instincts made him dodge out of Luke's grasp, and he was away.

Linas dropped the bottle of vodka he had just stolen and legged it down the street. Luke ducked through the gap and started to chase. Several holidaymakers were in the way and a woman screamed.

Linas was fast and nimble. He'd been a good runner in his youth and could dodge between people and get away from his pursuer easily. Luke, however, was still young and fit. His dream of joining the police meant he kept in shape at all times. Luke was confident he could catch up with Linas, and by the end of the road, right outside the amusement arcade on the seafront, he did. He grabbed him around the neck and pulled him down. It wasn't a rugby tackle as such, but it didn't matter; he got him to the ground.

As Linas struggled, Luke managed to press the red button on his Airwave radio set. This meant that there would be ten seconds of open mic, which would be broadcasted to all local units, and it would be recorded in case it was unintelligible.

'I have caught suspect for Op Dundee outside the arcade on the seafront. Need assistance,' Luke called as clearly as he could.

Within seconds sirens started up, sounding a long way away to Luke as he struggled with Linas, but which must have actually been quite near, since two PCs were running towards him a few minutes later.

In what felt like an instant Linas was handcuffed, and one of the officers had already radioed to the custody centre that there was a prisoner coming in.

Luke sat on the roadside looking at the state of his boots and trousers from the tussle, not really taking in what had happened.

'Have you got a thing about buying cakes?' he heard from behind him.

It was Michael Jones, who had heard the radio call and had come down to collect him. He had guessed rightly that in all the excitement of arresting the suspect everyone would forget about the PCSO. He had a grin on his face that Luke had never seen before.

'You are going to be flavour of the month with MCT forever after that little stunt!' he said, as Luke climbed into the car.

CHAPTER THIRTY-ONE

Crofts was having one of those mornings where nothing seemed to be going right. He had arrived in the office early, as he was duty senior this morning and had to oversee the tasking of the SOCOs by the control room. Many years ago, they had had their own controllers, so that their jobs were organised by operators who did this all the time. With the austerity cuts, those members of staff had been lost, meaning that it now fell to the supervisors to do, along with the hundred and one other tasks their role entailed. Crofts had to weigh up which jobs would take priority, which areas needed the most staff, and on top of it all, check how many staff would actually be physically working that day.

The long list of staff who were sick, on training courses or had other reasons for non-availability meant that he had very few examiners left to carry out all the work. As usual, there were going to be problems covering all the requests, especially as he had removed Hannah and Leighton from the roster, so they could continue to work on Op Dundee. Crofts spent twenty minutes making sure everything was covered for the eight o'clock shift and then grabbed the mugs from the desks of the staff due on duty that morning, mentally going through how everyone liked their teas and coffees. He headed round to the tea point, a small room with a sink, fridge and water boiler. *So much easier than the old days of boiling kettles*, he thought as he started making the drinks.

Making the teas was an age-old ritual within the police that had caused problems in recent years. From as far back as anyone could remember, the probationary constables – those just joining the force – had always made the teas at the beginning of each shift. They would continue to do so until someone new joined and then it would be their turn. However, in recent years, some new probationers had refused to do it. Firstly, because a lot of them had been to university and seen some of the world before joining and weren't as young and fresh-faced as some of their predecessors, and secondly because a lot of younger people didn't drink tea and coffee. This had led to them asking, why should I? The answer that it was something that had always been done wasn't good enough, and there had been refusals, causing uproar amongst the old and bold. Just another example of how 'the job was going down the pan'.

Crofts had never worried about things like that and had always taken a turn in making the drinks. He carried the steaming cups round to the office as the first members of staff started arriving.

In the far corner sat Paula Shadwell, the SSA – or scientific support assistant to give her full title. She was crucial to the running of the SOCO base. She carried out all the admin work, from ordering equipment and stores to preparing the lab submissions and countless other tasks, most of which weren't on her job description. Paula always drank a 'fancy' coffee that she brought in herself. Pleased he had remembered to use this, he hoped it would help make a pleasant start to the day for her.

Crofts asked her to come and see him when she was ready,

as he had some tasks for her concerning the submissions that had been sent off from Op Dundee. Paula said that she would ring the Forensic Recovery Unit as soon as someone would be in.

Crofts then spoke to the other SOCOs and told them what their initial tasks were for the day. Hannah and Leighton were to wait until after the briefing before heading off, just to check whether things had changed in the enquiry. He then walked around to the briefing room as the morning's updates began.

The main piece of news was the fact that the suspect, Belikas, had been seen in Hastings the day after the death. That was obviously good, as it meant that he hadn't fled and was probably still in the area, meaning it was only a matter of time before he was caught.

Crofts gave an update on their activity at the scene the day before and said that there should be some forensic results later that day. He also informed everyone that once the suspect was arrested, the forensic strategy would require samples from him.

Mead gave the final summary and thanked everyone for their work and sent them on their way.

Crofts headed back to the office. He could tell from the look on Paula's face as he approached her desk that there wasn't much good news to come.

'I contacted the FRU and got the answer that the syringe hasn't been chemically treated yet,' she told Crofts.

'What? It's been with them for two days. Surely it should have been done by now.'

Paula nodded. 'That's what I thought as well.'

'Don't worry, I'll call their manager,' Crofts told her as he walked over to his office. There was no need to look round at the inevitable rolling of eyes. None of the SOCOs were overly impressed with the service they got from that department. It mainly boiled down to the merger between Surrey's and Sussex's forensic services five years before. Whenever anything went wrong, the other force was always thought to be at fault, and as the FRU was in Surrey, the Sussex staff blamed everything on them.

Crofts closed the door and rang the manager's number. The phone was answered quickly by Dan Smithers. Crofts knew him fairly well because he'd been a senior SOCO in Surrey before the merger, so after a quick hello he launched straight into his complaint about the lack of results. Dan told him that the syringe had been swabbed for DNA, and it had been sent off to the forensic lab. It had then been treated for fingerprints, but there had been a problem with the superglue machine, which was why they were still awaiting the results. An engineer had fixed it, but it was being given a run-through before being used on this particular exhibit. Hopefully it would be processed in the next hour or so.

Crofts thanked him and made it clear that this exhibit needed treating as a priority, as the results could mean the difference between whether this enquiry was going to continue to be dealt with as a murder or not. Dan apologised again and assured Crofts that it would and that he would phone him personally with the findings.

Crofts put the phone down and thought about the situation. It couldn't be helped, and the result shouldn't be too long in coming, after all. He knew that superglue was the best chemical treatment for fingerprints on a plastic surface. It had been discovered by accident in the early eighties when a technician using superglue had spilt some. It was only later that he had realised the remaining superglue had reacted with the latent fingerprints, enhancing them.

Subsequent tests – some of them quite dangerous, looking

back – had found that heating superglue made it give off fumes which would enhance any fingerprints left on a plastic surface. A yellow dye had later been added, meaning the fingerprints would stand out even better.

Eventually machines had been developed which controlled the amount of heat and gave proper ventilation and safe extraction of the fumes. It had become an excellent way of recovering fingerprints, especially on plastic carrier bags, bin liners, plastic bottles and, of course, syringes.

Paula knocked on the door and told Crofts that she had spoken to Cellmark, one of the forensic service providers, and that they should be able to give him the results of the DNA work that afternoon. Crofts smiled with relief. It was funny that a company all the way over in Oxfordshire could give a result at the same time as a department in their own force, despite it taking a day longer to get the exhibits there and the techniques used being more complex. He reminded himself again not to be so cynical.

When the government closed the forensic science service back in 2012, a few of the smaller providers had expanded their work, albeit mainly with scientists who originally came from the FSS. In a competitive world these companies had had to make sure their services were good, and time frames were always the clients' biggest complaint about the FSS, so Cellmark made sure that its results were usually prompt.

A cup of tea had arrived on his desk. Crofts looked over and Leighton gave him a thumbs up. Crofts liked it when he had tea drinkers on duty, though sometimes, he ended up drinking too much.

He had just started going through some of the annual leave requests on the system when his mobile rang. Alison Williams, the deputy SIO.

'Good news. We've arrested Belikas,' she said.

He could hear the excitement in her voice. Crofts asked how it had happened, and Alison recounted the events and how Luke Smith had been involved in both episodes.

'I know who you mean,' Crofts said. 'He came on an attachment with us a couple of weeks ago, and he was so keen. Shame there aren't more like him. Anyway, I believe the suspect will be taken to Hastings' custody centre. The strategy is already in place, so if you let me know when the medical examiner is in the building, I will get a SOCO to meet them there. I won't send one now, as it will mean they'll be hanging around forever.'

Alison said she would.

Crofts knew from experience that it would take some time before everything was ready. Once arrested and taken to the custody centre, the prisoner needed a solicitor to be organised. Once they arrived, the solicitor would need time to speak to their client. The custody sergeant would then need to contact a superintendent to ask for their permission for the medical samples requested. The prisoner and the solicitor had time to decide whether to agree to those samples. It was within the prisoner's rights to refuse to give samples if they wanted to. Finally, once all was agreed, they would call a forensic medical examiner. The fact that all these people had to travel to Hastings would also add to the length of time needed. Altogether, it would often take hours before everyone was ready for the medical. Crofts had given up trying to work out how many SOCO working hours had been wasted sitting around in custody centres. What he did nowadays was put someone on standby who was in the area carrying out other work. He didn't have enough staff to do anything else.

He looked at the duty rota and smiled. The first thing that

had gone right today. Ellen Parsons was on a late shift that afternoon and was starting her shift in Hastings, as she lived over that way. She would be perfect for the task. Crofts sent her an email and a text to call him when she booked on and then sat back and enjoyed the rest of his cuppa.

Today was finally looking better.

CHAPTER THIRTY-TWO

Emily Collins was already out on patrol in Eastbourne town centre when she picked up another job over her Samsung handset. She'd been a PCSO in the town for about nine months now, and was used to getting tasks such as this whilst out and about.

When she saw that it was to do with a misper from the Foyer, she just shrugged. She had been there twice in the last fortnight, and both times the teenagers had returned within hours, but she left the shopping precinct and walked towards the Foyer. Emily just hoped that the duty manager was different from the last one she had met. He'd been really creepy, and she didn't like the way he looked at her.

She was a bit disappointed by the fact that she had to leave the busy shopping area, as that was where Emily enjoyed her job the most. Interacting with the public was what she liked and what she excelled at. Although only petite, she felt bigger with her uniform on and loved meeting the cross section of people around the town. She also loved helping people. Emily had recently decided she didn't want to become a police officer after all, as she had seen what they sometimes had to deal with, but her current role suited her down to the ground.

Emily was stopped several times by members of the public – one looking to find a taxi, another wanting to know the way to the theatre. She also had time to tell one of the street drinkers she had got to know that he was in a prohibited area. He knew but gave her a toothless smile and a mock bow, apologising and calling her 'Missy' before going on his way. Emily smiled to herself. Who would have thought a year ago, when she was working on the tills in Tesco, that she would be able to deal with something like that, and do it as simply as that?

Her confidence had grown day by day during the first few weeks, and Emily now found she enjoyed being out on independent patrol, as she could be herself more.

She finally got to the Foyer and used the intercom. The door was buzzed open. When she entered the hallway, two teenagers spotted her, stopped talking and disappeared up the stairs out of the way. What an effect she had on certain people. She laughed to herself, but her good mood was shattered when she saw that the duty manager was the same one. Emily felt him undress her with his eyes in the seconds that it took her to walk into his office. She blushed and knew he had spotted her.

Ronnie Jackson seemed to be trying to keep the look of lust out of his eyes but was failing miserably.

'I understand that you have reported a young girl as missing,' she said professionally.

'Yes,' Ronnie replied. 'And before you say anything about how many times you come here on a wasted journey, this one is different.'

'In what way?'

'For a start, she's never done this kind of thing before. She also has a job, which she enjoys, and never misses a shift, and this is so out of character for her. Her boss has called with the same concerns.'

'Right, let's get some details so that I can start circulating her description. When was the last time she was seen here?' Emily asked.

Ronnie said he had seen her before she went to work and that she had also completed her shift at The Moorings, but hadn't been seen since.

'So, you were the last person to see her from here?' Emily said. She noticed that Ronnie gave her an odd look as he realised what she was saying.

'Yes, I was, but as I said, she then went to work and was there all day.'

'So, no one knows whether she came back here after work or not,' Emily said as formally as she could. She knew Ronnie was now on the back foot and she was in charge.

'We don't keep full control on people's comings and goings, as everyone is meant to be treated as adults here. I only noticed her missing because she is always on time going to work in the mornings, unlike some, and because her boss called, as she knew it was out of character. I checked in her room after twenty-four hours, and there's nothing obvious in there to say she was planning to leave. I can take you up to her room for a look if you'd like.'

Emily could think of nothing worse than to be in a bedroom alone with this man.

'No, it's okay. I will pass the details on to CID when I get back, and they will continue with anything like that. It's not really my remit to go any further with the investigation.'

'Okay,' Ronnie said, disappointment in his voice.

'Do you have a photograph of Bethany?'

'Only this one from her file here,' Ronnie said.

'That will do, although that looks a little out of date.'

'No, she is really small in size and young looking. That was only taken last year.'

'Okay, I will contact The Moorings and speak to this Sandy and then hand the investigation over when I get back to base,' Emily told him, and then she left the Foyer as fast as she could.

She started to walk back towards the patrol centre, mulling over the information she had just received. It did sound different to the missing persons she had dealt with in the past. The fact that the duty manager was creepy hadn't helped the situation, but it was also because Bethany wasn't one of their usual runaways.

CHAPTER THIRTY-THREE

E llen Parsons had finally been called down to the custody centre for the medical. She had booked on duty at three and was told about the task, and Crofts had then emailed a copy of the strategy over to her. All normal run-of-the-mill stuff for a medical of this type, she had thought. She had then spoken to Crofts on the phone and had had an update on the job in general. She then got all the necessary kit ready and made a coffee and waited.

It was, in fact, a shorter wait than usual, mainly because the nurse was already dealing with someone in the custody block, so it was only the solicitor and the superintendent's authority that were needed. A translator had also been requested, and because of the number of Eastern Europeans locally, again there was already one in the station. The solicitor had spoken to his client and they had agreed to all the samples needed.

Ellen imagined that, due to the circumstances in this case, it had been a simple conversation, as there would be little evidence needed from Belikas's samples.

In the custody centre's medical room the smell was the same

as always, a mixture of body odours, dirty clothing and a vague hint of disinfectant.

'Wonderful!' Ellen said out loud as she went into the room, knowing she wouldn't get used to it even though she was going to be in there for the next hour or so.

Having put on her PPE and set up her camera and lenses, Ellen prepared the medical kits that would be needed during the examination. The door opened and in walked Suzanne Winter, the nurse. Ellen smiled – a mixture of friendliness and relief, as they knew each other well and had worked together before.

The two women had a quick chat about the job and what each would be doing, stopping when the custody assistant knocked on the door to ask if everything was ready for the prisoner.

Ellen replied that it was, and a minute later Linas walked in wearing a white coverall, the same as Ellen's. His clothing had been taken and packaged when he arrived in custody. Ellen looked at him with pity. Here was a young man ruined by drugs, which had led him here. How different could his life have been? She had given up wondering what the answers to these questions were after all these years.

The solicitor was a young bespectacled man whom Ellen hadn't met before. She could see that he was nervous – he was probably in this situation for the first time, she guessed – and he was also trying to project an air of authority but was failing. She and Suzanne shared a quick glance, and a slightly raised eyebrow was all that was needed for them to acknowledge their thoughts were the same.

Both were professionals, so they let him lead with a full formal statement of what his client was and wasn't going to do. Ellen was dying to butt in with a 'Listen, sunshine, he's actually charged with murder, so there's not a lot he could disagree with', but she bit her tongue and let the young man finish off his prologue.

Once the solicitor had stopped talking, Suzanne said, 'Right, young man, let's get started' a little too quickly, and Ellen saw the solicitor grimace and start to say something but change his mind. Linas was then stood against the plain wall, and Ellen started taking photos of him fully clothed from the front, then the side and then the rear.

Afterwards, Suzanne started an examination of all areas of his body, recording every blemish, spot, scar and mark. Obviously, since he was a drug user, there were a lot of syringe marks, and these were all recorded too. Ellen then photographed every item.

Once that was finished, Suzanne took all the swabs requested in the forensic strategy – DNA touch swabs from all areas of his skin, and other swabs from his mouth and also his hands.

Finally, she told him that swabs were needed of his genital and anal areas. The solicitor asked why, and Ellen explained that at that particular time there was no way of knowing what had happened and how his client was involved in the crime. If anything of a sexual nature happened during or in the run-up to the crime, these swabs could prove or disprove his involvement. The solicitor tried to make out that he knew that, and he was happy with it, although he didn't fool either of the women.

After taking the swabs, the final task was to take a sample of blood. This was needed for two reasons: firstly, to give a complete blood sample for DNA purposes, and secondly to give a reading for toxicology. Even though it was a long time after the event, the scientists could later count back to what levels of drugs were in his body at the time of the offence.

Once the medical was finished, Linas was taken back to his cell, and the solicitor thanked them for their work before going off to see his client. Ellen and Suzanne gave him time to get far enough away before both started laughing.

'Who did he think he was?' said Suzanne.

'Not quite sure,' said Ellen. 'I think he thought he was going to be running the show, but we soon showed him!'

'Oh dear,' said Suzanne, composing herself. 'I thought I was going to burst out laughing when he started!'

'I know, it was so funny. Just glad I could keep it in – I almost weed myself!' gasped Ellen, and both started laughing again.

They only stopped when the door opened, and they saw the custody assistant standing there, smiling.

'Dear me, I could hear you down the corridor!' he exclaimed.

The two women started again.

'Anyway, which one of you is Ellen?' he asked. She smiled and put her hand up like a schoolgirl.

'There's a phone call for you at the inspector's desk. Someone's been trying to get hold of you for a while, but obviously there's no signal down here for your mobile.'

Ellen walked along to the inspector's desk just as a local drunk began performing in the custody area and causing a commotion as the arresting officers stood by. His singing and dancing stopped abruptly when he saw Ellen, still wearing her white coverall.

'Oh my God, I've seen a ghost,' he announced, startled. He paused long enough for the officers to grab hold of him and drag him into a cell to sober up.

Ellen entered the inspector's office and picked up the phone, which was lying on the desk.

'Hello, mate, it's Crofty,' she heard from the other end. 'Have you started the medical yet?'

'Just finished,' Ellen replied. 'What's the problem?'

'Just got the results back from the lab. There's only the victim's DNA on the syringe that was in his arm, and then we also found out from the FRU that there is some ridge detail on that syringe, and although it wouldn't be enough on its own for an ident, there's enough there to say that it is from the victim too, so no trace of your man on it at all.'

'He's not my man!' Ellen corrected him quickly.

'You know what I mean,' Crofts replied. 'So, I've been along to see Tom Mead, and he's agreed that there is no evidence to keep your man in custody, so he can be released, and because of that Op Dundee is no longer a murder enquiry and the case will be dealt with by the coroner. So it's a big "stand down" to everyone.'

'Great. So, I've just wasted four hours of my life on that!' Ellen replied.

'Not as much time as the rest of us have collectively over the last couple of days!' Crofts answered.

'It makes you wonder why we bother on cases like this.'

'You know the answer. I've said it loads of times ... Because it's our job!' said Crofts. 'If you get yourself sorted and get over here quick enough, I'll make you a cup of tea.'

'Thanks, boss!' replied Ellen, with a hint of sarcasm that she knew Crofts would notice. 'I'm on my way.'

CHAPTER THIRTY-FOUR

E mily Collins decided it was an important enough call that she should go straight back to the patrol centre. It only took her twenty minutes to walk there; it was that quiet early evening time when most folks were home from work, having dinner and generally not needing to contact the police. It still amazed her that the reports of crime and general work levels rose and fell at almost the same times each day. Before joining she would never have guessed that.

Having let herself in through the security gate, she buzzed herself through into the main building. She phoned Sandy at The Moorings and got the same story as Ronnie had given her and the same concern. Bethany appeared to be someone who was always on time and never missed a shift.

Emily walked over to the CID area of the patrol room. It was all just one large room. Several years ago the police had decided that open-plan offices were the way forward, and this building had become one. Each area of the room was identical except for the colour of the chairs, which were red, green, purple or yellow. Not many liked the open-plan set-up. It was quite noisy at times and felt crowded, but the good thing was that officers in each area were more approachable. Especially the CID.

There had always been a mystique surrounding that department. In the old days junior officers would be scared to enter that hallowed area of the building. Nowadays that barrier wasn't there, as everyone was just a desk apart. As she approached, Emily could see about half a dozen detectives, all either on the phone or staring at their computer screens.

She wasn't too sure who to speak to at first, but then recognised DC Clare Perks putting down her phone in anger and shaking her fist at the plastic object. Clare laughed when she noticed the concern on Emily's face.

'Bloody CPS. You couldn't make it up. They've just dropped charges on a burglary that we have found fingerprints at because the suspect said he had legitimate access to the building as he once worked there as a painter!'

Probably noticing that Emily was looking a little apprehensive, she softened.

'Sorry, darling, how can I help?'

Emily relaxed. She had met Clare several times whilst on attachments and liked the way she called everyone by the same term of endearment. It made her feel welcome.

Emily talked through the story of the missing girl. Clare listened with interest, although Emily did see a hesitation when she first mentioned the Foyer, but Emily soon recovered her composure when she explained the different circumstances. She told Clare everything she knew so far and then finished with a pause. Clare, who was a trained interviewer, must have realised that there was something else that Emily wasn't sure about.

'Go on,' she said in a friendly manner. 'I'm still listening.'

'It's just about the duty manager there, Ronnie Jackson. I've always felt there's something creepy about him. It's the way he looks at me when I go there,' she added hesitantly, expecting Clare to laugh.

'Don't worry about him. If he looks at me like that, he'll get a swift kick in the bollocks!' Clare replied.

'If that's not enough, he was the last person to see her in the Foyer. She did go to work that day, but I still think it's a coincidence, or maybe it's just me overthinking.'

'Don't ever stop doing that, darling,' Clare replied in her soothing manner. 'My old DI used to say that there's such a thing as a gut instinct and that all detectives should use it. It has certainly helped me over the years.'

Emily relaxed. Clare changed screens on her computer and told Emily to sit down as she typed in Bethany's name. As expected, her name came up with a couple of cautions from when she was younger. Clare then put the Foyer into the system, but it threw up too many hits.

Lastly, she tried Ronnie Jackson's name. All appeared clear to start with, but then she noticed that there were historical notes, so she read them and saw that he had been questioned several times by police but never charged. It was when she noted that these incidents concerned children, from when he had been a teacher, that alarm bells started ringing. Clare had spent five years on child protection and could spot a paedophile easily. She also knew that the reporting of that type of crime had been pretty lax back then, and that many paedophiles had been able to continue for years before the police got their act together.

It also worried her that a man such as this was now working for an establishment for young people.

'Do you have a picture of Bethany?'

Emily handed it over, and Clare repeated exactly what Emily had said about her looking young.

'No, she looks like that. It was only taken last year.'

Clare gulped: those alarm bells were getting louder.

Clare made up her mind straight away. 'Right, darling, let me go for a quick ciggie, then I'll grab a car and you can come with me down to the Foyer. I'd like to meet this Mr Jackson, even if it's only to see if he fancies me!' she said, laughing.

Emily was very happy with this outcome. Not only did someone believe her suspicions, but she was actually going to be taken along for part of the investigation.

CHAPTER THIRTY-FIVE

Linas wasn't quite sure what was happening. He had agreed to everything the solicitor had asked for through the interpreter and had watched as the irritating man had tried to show the women dressed in white paper suits that he was in charge. Linas had noticed that he had failed too. In fact, if he hadn't been in such a serious situation, he probably would have laughed at him as well. However, he wasn't going to at this moment because he needed his help. He was happy to go along with anything that was asked, as he knew he was innocent. His old friend had died from whatever he had taken, and Linas knew it wasn't his fault.

At the end of the medical, he had been taken back to a cell whilst the solicitor tried to organise a bail application. Linas had sat and wept again at the thought of what had happened in the last two days, his memories of Jonny, and of how bad his life was in general.

How had it come to this? He had originally travelled to the UK for work, and he was happy to do anything. Linas had worked hard, and although the money had been poor, he had made enough to keep himself going. He couldn't remember when he had got into substance misuse, and he couldn't think why he had, but he knew it wasn't how he had planned his life.

He was just going over it all again when the cell was unlocked, and the solicitor entered with a beaming smile. Linas couldn't make out what he was saying at first, but it sounded like he was being freed. He asked the solicitor to slow down, as he was getting overexcited and speaking too fast. He then heard what the solicitor was saying.

He was being released because there was no evidence against him.

Linas slumped back down on the bench in the cell, a mixture of relief and elation together with the sadness for his friend all rolled together. The tearfulness from a few minutes ago now grew into full-on crying, sobbing and wailing. The solicitor didn't know what to do.

The noise attracted one of the custody assistants out in the corridor. He popped his head round the door and asked if there was anything he could do to help.

The solicitor just stood there, staring and looking pleadingly at him. The assistant, who was used to dealing with prisoners all day long, knew exactly what was needed. He went and spoke to the custody sergeant who agreed with his request, and then he got straight on the phone to the East Sussex drug and alcohol recovery service, better known as STAR. Someone from STAR promised to be in touch right away.

The assistant went back into the cell and explained it all to Linus and to the solicitor. Within the hour an advisor would be along for a chat with Linas. The organisation could give him counselling for his addiction and for his grief. They could also help him find somewhere to stay temporarily, and depending on how Linas reacted to their programme, could maybe even find him somewhere for good.

Linas couldn't believe what he was hearing. For the first

time in many months, it sounded like someone wanted to help him. He was overjoyed and told them both that he was happy to go along with anything offered. He had already decided that it was time for a change in his attitude to the world, and here were people offering support.

Poor Jonny's demise was going to lead to a new life for Linas. He would never forget him.

CHAPTER THIRTY-SIX

Suzie was harassed. She'd had another one of those days with the twins. It seemed that every day was like this at the moment. She did love them but at the same time hated how much her life had changed. It really didn't suit her being a mummy. Some of the other girls she met absolutely loved it all, but Suzie didn't.

The only good news today was that, for some reason, Stevie was coming back early this week; in fact, he was due home soon. That meant he could take over the hassle of looking after the little angels. She had already phoned Naomi Ashworth to arrange a trip to the spa for them the next day at a local country club they used to frequent a lot more before the twins were born. Naomi had sounded relieved to hear from Suzie; it appeared that being married to Freddie wasn't always fun, and she needed a girly day out too.

The twins were actually being quiet, amusing themselves with their toys, for once. Stevie wouldn't believe it, but it was the first time it had been like this all day. They had probably tired themselves out with all their crying and screaming. It had started at breakfast, after a night interrupted by one or the other crying. Neither wanted to eat; all they wanted to do was throw their food at one another, which then started the other crying. Suzie had had enough. She washed and dressed them through more tears and then plonked them in the back of the Range Rover before taking them into town. She thought that a morning shopping for new clothes for them would cheer them up; unfortunately, it didn't. Suzie had yet to realise that shopping was boring for her little ones and probably one of their least favourite things to do. So she continued, all the time wondering why there was so much crying.

Whenever Stevie took them out, there wasn't any crying. Probably because he didn't drag them round the shops. They cried and cried then made Suzie agitated and embarrassed, which meant she took them home again.

She didn't understand that all they needed was a little attention like all children.

She heard the car pull up before the twins did.

'Daddy's home,' she called out to them.

The playing stopped as they looked at each other, and a grin appeared on each of their faces, the first that Suzie had seen that day.

'Daddy, Daddy!' they called in unison at the sound of Stevie's car door slamming shut outside. They could see him through the large window of the barn conversion that was their home. He had spotted them too and was waving to them with a silly smile on his face.

Stevie grabbed his bag out of the boot of the car and headed into the hallway. He hadn't even had time to put the case down before his little munchkins had run to him and were hugging his legs. He reached down and picked one up in each arm, kissing them both one after the other.

'How are my two favourite children today?' he asked.

They replied with another 'Daddy, Daddy!' and more kisses.

He had certainly missed them and knew his plans were right. He looked to the doorway of the room, where Suzie was standing. He noticed the look on her face; it wasn't one of love but relief. Not about seeing him but because he would now be taking over the childcare duties for the next few days.

It annoyed him, but he decided not to say anything for now. He could save that for later, when the time was right.

He called 'Hello, sweetheart' to her and saw her pull herself together as she walked over and offered him her cheek, which he dutifully kissed. As he did, he realised it wasn't a proper loving kiss, just a peck, which Suzie didn't seem too upset about.

'I haven't bathed the twins, as I know you like to do that,' she told him stiffly.

'No problem,' Stevie replied, knowing she wouldn't have anyway.

'I thought we could order a takeaway tonight seeing as we hadn't planned on you being here.'

'Fine,' he answered, knowing it would have been a takeaway tonight even if she had known he was coming home. Cooking wasn't at the top of the list of Suzie's domestic talents. He sometimes wondered whether she had any domestic talents at all.

'Indian or Chinese?' she asked quickly, probably realising what Stevie was thinking.

'I'll have a curry for a change,' he replied. 'Haven't had one for a while.'

Suzie went off to the kitchen to order, and Stevie carried the twins upstairs for their bath and the remainder of their preparation for bedtime.

Someone once told him that children loved routine and that you needed to get them into one as soon as possible. He always made sure he did just that, and had found that they enjoyed it, and it also made them settle easily. It was another thing Suzie struggled with, and he had lost count of the number of times she had phoned him up at about ten at night with the sound of the twins crying in the background while he was away. It made him feel guilty but, at the same time, he wondered why she would let it get to that stage.

He ran the bath, looking at all of the new toys that had appeared whilst he had been away, and then went into their bedroom, noticing new clothes still on their hangers dotted around the room. Suzie still knew how to shop, even though it wasn't all for her.

In fact, Stevie hadn't realised there was designer clothing for children until Suzie had found it. She now managed to add that to her never-ending list of purchases. The bath was ready and the bubbles were plenty, so he told the twins to choose one toy each to take into it with them. He saw a look pass between the two of them, as they decided whether to challenge him, but it was over in a second. Stevie was still getting used to the fact that even at this age there seemed to be some type of twin perception. Henry chose a dinosaur and Aimee a pony. Both then skipped into the bathroom, where Stevie helped undress them before putting them into the bubbly, warm bath.

Having made sure they were fully washed, Stevie launched into a made-up tale involving Henry, Aimee, a pony and a dinosaur, giving the characters their own individual voices. This is what the twins loved the most, something that their mother never did with them. The story took them into a fantasy land where the pets were led through a forest made of bubbles that would suddenly splash and land on Stevie's head, something that gave them fits of laughter every time. In fact, the twins were so involved they weren't fully listening to the story, just waiting for the pile of suds to land on his head. Their beaming faces, with wet hair plastered down, made them look even more gorgeous than ever, and Stevie marvelled once again at how lucky he was to have been blessed with these two.

After about half an hour of fun and frolics, it was time for the plug to be pulled and for all of the bubbles to be sucked away by the bubble monster, and then it was time to dry them both and put their pyjamas on. He called for Suzie to warm up some milk and then settled down on the settee in their room with a book and an arm around each of them.

Suzie came in with their bottles. Stevie could see she was annoyed, as she could never get them like this on her own. She sniffed and went off to have a shower. She had, Stevie noticed, forgotten to come and give them both a kiss goodnight, but it didn't seem to bother them too much as they both listened intently to the story while drinking their warm milk. He continued for twenty minutes, noticing that both were slowly nodding off.

Stevie made sure that they were ready and then put them in their beds, promising to continue the story once they were all tucked in. This he did, and both were asleep within five minutes. Easy, he thought as he turned off their lamps, leaving just a night light on in the room, which for a split second reminded him of the room in the Travelodge.

He shook that thought out of his mind. That was all done and dusted. Now Stevie was about to face one of the most difficult conversations he had had for a long time. He grabbed a quick shower, put on some tracksuit bottoms and a T-shirt and walked down the stairs to see Suzie.

CHAPTER THIRTY-SEVEN

Ronnie Jackson was in the office and just coming to the end of his shift when he saw the two women on the CCTV. His excitement at seeing Emily again was soon curtailed by his first look at Clare Perks. Even though he had yet to meet her, he didn't like her demeanour. Ronnie wondered whether he could call Josie to take over, as she had already arrived and was in the staffroom, but then realised it would look like he was trying to avoid them, and Josie would realise that – and anyway, he had nothing to hide. He buzzed them through on the intercom, and they came around to the office.

As soon as she walked in, Clare made up her mind that her initial thoughts about him were true, and she didn't trust him.

Ronnie gave the two of them an overeager welcome, which didn't sound natural, and it made him appear even stranger. He tried to speak to Emily to start with but Clare interrupted.

'I understand from Emily here that one of your inmates is missing.'

Ronnie ignored Clare's blatant dig at the residents.

'Yes, she went to work yesterday morning, did a full shift at The Moorings and hasn't been seen since.'

'Allegedly,' snapped Clare.

'What do you mean?' he asked.

'Well, you are saying she hasn't been seen since, but someone must've seen her. People don't disappear into thin air!'

'Oh yes, I see what you mean,' Ronnie replied nervously.

'Emily says that you were the last person to see her leave here,' she said forcefully. Not giving him time to reply, Clare continued, 'What was she like when you saw her that morning?'

'She seemed fine. She left the same time she always does. She is very conscientious and never misses work for anything, and that is why we are worried about her. It's not like some of the other guests here. She's not the type to run away.'

Clare didn't take her eyes off him as he spoke, and she could see he was unnerved by this, which was good, as it gave her the upper hand. Her years of experience of interviewing all types of suspects meant she wasn't scared of any man in this situation; she was in charge.

'You say Bethany is a creature of habit, so do you know what time she returns at night?' she asked.

'Usually just before eleven. She gets the bus from Pevensey Bay to the station and then walks from there.'

'And did she do that that night?'

'I'm not sure, as I wasn't on duty that evening.'

'But you would have known when she was due.'

'Yes,' said Ronnie, not quite sure what she was trying to insinuate but not liking her tone of questioning.

'So, would whoever was on duty have made a note of whether she arrived or not?' Clare asked, almost ignoring his response.

'Not really. We don't check our guests in and out all the time; it's just certain ones that you notice. Mainly with Bethany because she is always on time.'

'Was there another reason you knew so much about her?'

'What do you mean?' Ronnie asked anxiously.

'Nothing. Let's go and see her room,' Clare ordered him rather than asked him.

Ronnie didn't like this woman at all. He felt intimidated by her and almost dropped the keys as he took them from the hook.

Clare spotted it but didn't show that she had. She looked at Emily, who smiled back. Emily was certainly enjoying the way Clare was dealing with Ronnie. How she wished she could be that forceful.

At Bethany's room, Ronnie unlocked the door and stood back. It was small in there, and he didn't want to get anywhere near this woman; she was making him feel nervous.

Clare had a quick look around the room. It was very tidy and very empty. She opened the drawers and the wardrobe and had a quick look, careful not to disturb too much in case it needed looking at forensically later. There wasn't anything she could see that would be of use to her at this stage of the enquiry. She did, however, see a picture of Bethany in a frame on the side.

'Is that a recent picture of her?' she asked Ronnie.

He stepped into the room to check. 'Yes, it is.'

'Doesn't she look young?' Clare said.

'Yes, everyone says that,' he replied, stepping backwards out of the room but bumping his elbow on the door as he went out, making him wince with pain.

Again, Clare noticed but said nothing. 'So, she could be mistaken for a younger person quite easily, even a child.'

'Yes.'

'You used to be a teacher, didn't you?' Clare asked quietly.

Ronnie was shocked by the statement and knew it had shown on his face.

'Er, yes, a long time ago,' he replied, unsure why or how she knew.

'What made you give it up?' Clare asked as if she wasn't really interested.

'I realised it wasn't for me. I couldn't cope with the stress caused by naughty children.'

'So, you went into social work, where there were even more naughty kids.'

'Never really thought of it like that!' replied Ronnie, with a false laugh that hung in the air in the quiet of the room. 'I wanted to move to a career that helped people. I didn't enjoy teaching after all.'

'Oh.' Clare continued to look at him. 'I'll take that photograph so that we can circulate the picture as a missing person as soon as possible, and I'll take her toothbrush so that we have a control sample of her DNA in case we need it at any time.'

Ronnie was relieved that the conversation was over but still felt there was something worrying about her knowledge of him.

'We'll head back to the nick and get the photo sent out to all forces,' Clare said. 'It is more likely at this stage that she has just gone missing, especially with her background. She is one of the most vulnerable for that type of scenario. I'll also do some background checks to see if there is anything else that comes up.'

Ronnie wondered what type of checks these would be but decided it was something he wasn't going to ask her about. Clare sealed the toothbrush in an exhibit bag she had in her briefcase and waited for Ronnie to lock up and lead them back down to the office.

'Obviously, if you hear anything about Bethany from anyone, let us know so that we can cancel the misper report,' she told Ronnie when they got to the main entrance.

'No problem. I surely will,' he replied.

'I will be in touch as soon as I find anything,' she said as she and Emily started to leave the building.

She didn't need to turn round and see the look on Ronnie's face. Emily did, though, and loved what she saw.

The two of them walked towards the car. Some youths were hanging around outside the building, larking about and making a fair amount of noise. This stopped immediately when they spotted Clare and Emily. Emily knew this wasn't because of her, as she had never had that reaction from young people when she was out on her beat; it was due to Clare. Those youths knew who Clare was and that she wasn't for mucking about. Again, Emily wished she had that type of influence over people.

'What an arsehole!' Clare said, laughing, once they were in the car.

Emily joined in the laughter before replying, 'He wasn't like that with me!'

'I guessed that. I had him on the back foot all the time. I must admit the mention of his background really threw him, didn't it?'

'Yes, it certainly did,' said Emily. 'I didn't think you'd say anything about it.'

'I wasn't going to, but I didn't like the look of him, so I decided to just throw that one in there to see his reaction. I think there's certainly more to Mr Jackson than meets the eye, and I'm going to be looking into it. Whether or not he has anything to do with this job I can't tell you right now, but what I do know is that that man has something to hide.'

Emily relaxed into her seat. Not only had her instinct been right, but it now looked as though that awful man was going to get his comeuppance as well.

CHAPTER THIRTY-EIGHT

Suzie was glad Stevie had taken over the parenting as soon as he walked in. She had ordered the takeaway and had already opened a bottle of Prosecco. She could hear Stevie finish in the shower as she gulped down her second glass. The doorbell rang, and the delivery man from the Indian takeaway arrived with the food. Suzie thanked him and gave him a two-pound tip, which he received with a frown, glancing up at the large house that clearly showed she could afford more. Suzie didn't notice. She just shut the door, took the food in and retrieved two plates from the cupboard, which was almost as much as she could manage in the kitchen. She set up two places on the breakfast bar and waited for Stevie to finish upstairs.

He came down the stairs looking clean and fresh, and she remembered why she had been attracted to him in the first place. She hadn't done too badly, had she? Stevie said he was famished after a long day on the road and helped himself to a bottle of Bud from the fridge.

He went straight for the starters and ate two of the small onion bhajis, almost without chewing, and then set about opening the rest of the cartons spread out on the worktop.

Suzie's culinary skills didn't include serving up either, so they ate the food directly from the cartons as usual.

The next few minutes were taken up by serving, tasting and commenting on the curries. Stevie loved a good curry, and it was lucky that their local was one of the best around. Suzie, also enjoying the food, finished the last of the bottle of Prosecco. She opened another, poured herself a glass and sat down.

'You said you had something to tell me,' she said.

'Yes, I do,' replied Stevie. 'I've noticed that you haven't been enjoying being a mother. So I have been trying to think of a way that I could help you.'

Suzie was about to argue the first point and then realised there was more to come, so bit her lip.

'As you know, I've been very successful in my job over the last few years, even top salesman several times.'

'I know,' Suzie replied, remembering the great nights they'd enjoyed at top London restaurants and hotels to accept those awards.

'Well, I thought it was about time the company gave a little back to me, so I went and saw the regional manager while I was down that way, and he has offered me a promotion and an office-based job at their headquarters.'

'Sounds good, but where is their headquarters?' Suzie replied, slowly realising that this may affect her life.

'It's actually in Ashford, in Kent, but I was thinking we could move down to the coast somewhere. It would be great for the twins to grow up by the seaside.'

'I don't want to move down south. I hate the people,' she replied straight away. 'Everyone's a clever sod, and anyway, I like it here, all my friends are here, and we have a good life. Why would we want to go and spoil it all by moving to somewhere I don't like and where we don't know anyone?' She scoffed at him. 'That's a pathetic idea!'

Stevie took a breath. He had guessed she would say something like that. 'I think it's a great idea. Not only do I get a promotion, but I also get more settled hours and will be able to get home most evenings to help with the twins.'

'But that's not what I want!'

'What do you mean?' he asked, puzzled.

'I don't want you working as a medical rep, and I don't want to move away. I just want our life to be as it was when we were first together, you running businesses, and us enjoying ourselves. You have turned into Mr Boring, and I don't like it anymore!' she shouted.

Stevie sat in stunned silence. He wasn't really ready for that outburst, although it didn't completely surprise him.

'I thought I was doing the right thing bringing money in and thinking of the twins' future,' he said.

'What about my future?' Suzie replied almost hysterically. 'Have you thought of that?'

'Well, yes, I thought it would include me and the twins,' he said with genuine concern.

'Oh, I don't know,' she snapped with tears in her eyes. 'I don't think that is what I want.'

Stevie sat staring at her as she sobbed and tried to regain her composure. 'Well, if you think like that, then maybe I should leave and take the twins with me.'

Suzie started crying properly now. Stevie felt he should put his arm around her and give her a cuddle, but he didn't. He had just been told what he had known for some time, that Suzie didn't want to be with either him or the twins. It wasn't a surprise; it was just that he didn't think she would admit it.

Suzie picked up the bottle of Prosecco and her glass and, without saying another word, walked past him and went and sat in the lounge. She turned the TV on and chose a music channel. Stevie could see her from where he was and thought how pathetic she looked and how, within a few minutes, any love he still had for her had diminished. He knew this would be the beginning of the end of their marriage, but he also realised Suzie would have a lot of wants and needs and that he would have to be careful how he approached the subject.

The one thing he was sure of was that he would give those two children upstairs a better life on his own – better than with her.

He threw away the half-empty cartons and put the plates in the already full dishwasher and started it up, wondering why Suzie couldn't even carry out a simple task like that. He then poured himself a large glass of Cabernet Sauvignon and walked through to his den, where he sat down, put some headphones on, connected his iPhone and listened to some music.

CHAPTER THIRTY-NINE

Crofts was back on his bike the next morning, feeling a little more relaxed. He'd had another good night's sleep, having not been on call, and was ready for the day ahead. As he cycled along with U2's 'Gloria' blaring out on his headphones, he thought quickly about what he would be doing that day at work. Because Op Dundee had been downgraded to a coroner's case, he had a full day in the office, where he could catch up with all the admin that would have built up over the last few days while he was over in Hastings.

It was the only thing he didn't like about his job. All the day-to-day work he was expected to do in his role was hard enough as it was without having to postpone it whilst dealing with major crimes and then having to pick it all up again afterwards. He was proud of the fact that he was good at his job, but it annoyed him that in instances such as this, others might think he was inefficient, through no fault of his own.

He swiped himself in through the main gate of the patrol centre and put his bicycle in the rack. After removing his helmet but not his headphones, he looked up and noticed that Clare Perks was speaking to him whilst she stood having a ciggie at the nearby smoking point. He held his hand up to her and then stopped his music before apologising.

'Morning, Crofty,' she called. 'How do you fancy a decent job?'

He smiled. He had known Clare for years and guessed she was onto something.

'I could do without one today. I've got loads to catch up on after Op Dundee,' he replied with a smile.

'That wasn't a job, that was just a druggie death!' she said mockingly.

'I'll have you know the coroner expects all of those types of death to be treated as murder until proven otherwise,' he replied.

'I have a real job that will need a decent SOCO to deal with it.' Again, the mockery.

'What have you got then?' he asked.

'I've got a teenage girl who has gone missing – completely out of character, never done it before. I've been to see the manager of the place she lives at, and I'm not happy with him. The man's got a history which makes me believe he was a paedo, and I think he's hiding something. He's too nervous.'

'No wonder he's nervous with you on his case. Clare Perks, the only woman I know who can make grown men cry!' Crofts joked, referring to when Clare had indeed made a hardened criminal cry during an interview on a murder enquiry. Crofts had seen the video. It had been an excellent bit of interview work and had ended in a murder confession, something that didn't happen that often. It showed how good she was at her job, and Crofts could see that she liked the reference, even if she was pretending to ignore it.

'I'm going back to see him later, after I've done some more delving into his background,' she continued. 'If I'm still not happy with him, I'm going to nick him and bring him in for questioning. If I do, I'll need a forensic strategy for him and for the victim's address.'

'No problem,' replied Crofts. 'You've got my number. Where does she live?' he asked.

'I wasn't going to tell you, but ... it's the Foyer, and I know what you'll say.'

'I understand why. Never mind. Let me know what you need ... if anything.'

'See, I knew you would lose interest the moment I mentioned that place, but honestly, this is out of character. You know I wouldn't say anything if I didn't think it was a goer.'

'I know,' he replied. 'Keep in touch.' He nodded goodbye before entering the building and heading into the office.

CHAPTER FORTY

S uzie awoke with a banging headache, fully clothed on top of her bed. She couldn't remember going to bed. She steadied her thoughts, trying to recall what had happened last night, and let out a groan.

Suzie slowly remembered the conversation she had with Stevie about his promotion and the fact that she didn't want to move. What on earth would she want to do that for?

She then remembered the conversation about the twins. *Oh dear. That was maybe a little too much*, she thought. It was, however, how she felt. She didn't enjoy being a mum, and it did intrude into her life of lunches out with friends, pamper days and all the fun times she used to have before the children were born. Suzie also knew that Stevie was besotted with them and was happy to choose them over her.

He had made that perfectly clear over the last few months, spending every moment with them when he was finally at home for the weekend. In fact, she had noticed he was excluding her a lot of the time recently. Planning things for him and the twins that he knew she wouldn't want to join in with.

Through her pounding headache, Suzie realised what she

had done, making her feelings about their marriage and the twins clear to Stevie, and it looked like he was happy to go along with it. In fact, his ideas had made it an even better reason to split, as it would take them away from her and leave her to get back to her own life.

She hadn't really wanted kids in the first place. Having them had been his idea, and it had only been to try to save their marriage. It hadn't worked.

Suzie stretched and felt a smile cross her face. This was actually going to be a good thing after all. She was looking forward to her spa day with Naomi. Now she would have something to celebrate as well.

Maybe she should look up somewhere nice for them to eat. Her smile widened at the thought of a real girly day, the first of many to come. She almost drifted back off to sleep with that smile on her face but was woken by the squeal of one of the twins, who were downstairs playing with their dad. She couldn't remember whether he had slept in the bed with her or not overnight. It didn't matter anyway; their new lives meant that this was a thing of the past too.

It was then that a thought came into her mind which made her feel sick. If there was a divorce and Stevie moved away with the kids, where was she going to live, and what was she going to do to earn money? Since she had been with Stevie, she had never needed to work. He had always earned a lot of money whatever he had done. If they were getting divorced and he got custody of the twins, she wouldn't get anything. The house was rented, her car was on finance and all her cards were paid for by him.

'You stupid cow!' Suzie said out loud to herself. 'You haven't thought this through. If you agree to his plans, you'll end up with absolutely nothing.'

She realised then and there that she needed to fight dirty, to oppose everything, and then hopefully get a payout from Stevie; otherwise, she would end up with nothing. She needed to get him to plead with her to have them. She was making it too easy for him.

Suzie decided to change tactics. She hadn't got to where she had in life without pulling a few tricks over the years. She would still be living on that council estate if she hadn't become streetwise, and it was time to be so again.

She looked around the room. What could she start with? She spotted Stevie's wallet on the other bedside table. She didn't normally do this, as she had no need to, but maybe there was something in there she could use in her new quest. She knew he always kept his receipts, as he needed them for his claims and for his tax return, so there were always plenty in there. Maybe she could start making a note of them and pretend he was having an affair. That may help her story when it came to the solicitors.

She also thought she would be able to get Naomi to say some bad things about him. That would help. This plan was going to be easier than she had first thought. Especially as she was using underhand tactics, something Stevie would never think of.

Suzie looked through the receipts. They confirmed what he had told her he'd done over the last few days. Petrol receipts from both journeys, overnight stays in a Travelodge and a Premier Inn. 'Cheapskate!' she muttered. She wouldn't be seen dead in either establishment. Two other receipts for meals and that was it. Nothing she was going to be able to dish any dirt on him with. She needed to think harder.

She checked all of the credit cards, mentally making a note of them, as she knew she didn't have a lot of time; Stevie would be up soon to change to go out with his beloved twins for the day. She could look on the computer after Stevie had gone, search through his accounts, see where he might have made a mistake, find anything that could be used against him. She then remembered a story Naomi had told her about a friend called Rosie, who had hired a private detective to spy on her husband, as she thought he was up to something. He was, and with the evidence given by the private eye, she had ended up with a large amount of money.

Suzie was so glad she was having a spa treatment with Naomi today. Between them they would hatch a plan.

She was just putting the last leisure club card back in its slot in the wallet when something stopped it from sliding in properly. Puzzled, she looked inside the slot and saw a small piece of paper tucked away. Suzie took it out and read it. It was a receipt from left luggage at Victoria station dated a couple of days ago. She wondered what it was all about but had no time to dwell, as she heard Stevie tell the twins he was just going upstairs to change. She put the wallet back on the side, tucked the receipt in her bra and lay down, pretending to sleep, as he walked into the room.

'Oh, so you are awake,' Stevie said sarcastically.

'Yes, I am. I'm not feeling too good. It must have been that curry.'

'More likely the two bottles of Prosecco you had!' he scoffed.

Suzie didn't reply. She knew he wasn't that stupid.

'Me and the twins are going out for the day. I take it you don't want to come,' he said.

'I've arranged to meet up with Naomi. We don't normally manage to see each other during the week, so I thought it would make a change.'

'That's okay. We'll see you later. By the way, do you remember our conversation last night about the future?'

'Of course I do, and I can tell you I'm shocked by the whole thing,' she snapped. 'I can't believe you just want to finish our marriage and steal the twins from me. I'm going to fight you for them all the way. They usually give custody to the mothers anyway.'

'We'll see,' Stevie replied, moving away from her, hoping she hadn't seen the look on his face. Her reaction and comments last night had made him think it was all going to be easy. Obviously in the cold light of day Suzie had had a rethink. What had made her change her mind?

CHAPTER FORTY-ONE

Clare Perks had been busy. She had looked through many old-style written crime reports and cross-checked them against Jackson's name, but had come up with nothing. It was annoying her. She had found this a problem before, and it was all down to the way things had changed since the age of the computer.

Computers had made police work a hundred times more efficient. There had been several high-profile enquiries where it had been shown that the old ways of investigating were slow and laborious and had allowed killers to evade capture, the most significant being the Yorkshire Ripper case, back in the eighties. The images of the enquiry team manually checking through card indexes demonstrated how old-fashioned it had all been. It was events such as those which eventually led to the modern-day computer systems that were now in place for investigating crime.

Although computers were good at most things, there were problems when dealing with historic crimes. This was because the system was only as good as the inputter. The main problem was that when reports were recorded in the early days of computers and inputting, they were not done so as efficiently as they would be currently. On top of this was the problem that paedophiles had been largely unchallenged back in those days. The world was a different place then, and much of this activity had been kept hidden from view and had not been investigated properly, as it was now.

Most officers were aware that there were people around who "fancied" children, but it had been talked about in a jokey way and never really thought of seriously. This was the reason so many historic reports were currently being dealt with, as no one had taken these crimes seriously at the time.

Clare's work on the child protection unit meant she knew all the reasons why it was so hard to follow up on these people. She also knew there were other ways of catching them and that she was one of the best at it.

She was aware of Jackson's background and that he had some kind of history around young people and was now working amongst them. This was what started her thinking. The fact that he was now in a position of trust didn't matter to her, as that was a ploy that many paedophiles used. Clare wouldn't have made the connection just because Jackson worked at the Foyer; she had become suspicious when she saw how young Bethany looked in the photograph. Clare decided to talk it through with her detective sergeant, Bill Sellings. They had worked together over the years, both in child protection and in general CID. Bill was old school, a genial Geordie but also a very good detective and a good supervisor.

Clare made him a coffee and took it to him in his small, cramped office.

'What are you after, Ms Perks?' he asked. 'You making me a coffee without requesting means you're after something.'

Clare smiled and said she had a case that she was interested in but needed some guidance, and then told him all of what had happened so far.

'Sounds like this Jackson fella needs talking to,' Bill said.

'He does, but I don't have anything to arrest him for, and that is the problem at the moment.'

They both sat thinking it through, Bill sipping his coffee.

'I've got it!' he suddenly stated. 'We can bring him in, voluntarily, as a significant witness to Bethany's disappearance. Once we have him here, we can delve a little into his background and see what he comes up with.'

'What if he says no?'

'He's not likely to, is he? At this moment he'll just be "helping the police with their enquiries". He has nothing to hide in this situation so far. It's up to us to find out what he's really been up to, now and in the past.'

Clare smiled. She knew she could rely on Bill to come up with a solution.

'Shall I phone him and ask him to come in then?'

'No, let's just pop round and see him, and then we can invite him nicely while we're there. I always like to see the reaction on their face. It can often give us a clue as to what their demeanour is.'

'Sounds good to me. What time shall we go?'

'As soon as I've had another coffee. All this thinking is making me thirsty!' Bill replied with a wink.

'Looks like it's my turn again then, doesn't it?' Clare said, with a shake of her head as she gathered up the dirty cups. 'I suppose in these circumstances that I should, but if this turns out to be a runner, then I'll expect more than a coffee. Pinot Grigio is my current favourite!' She laughed.

'You're on!' Bill replied.

CHAPTER FORTY-TWO

Suzie arrived at the spa in a daze. It wasn't just the hangover. It was the fact that she couldn't believe the predicament she found herself in. She sat in the reception area waiting for Naomi and ran through what Stevie had said over and over in her mind. She was miles away when Naomi walked up to her.

'Hello, anyone in?' Naomi shouted, waving right in front of her.

Suzie came to with a jump and looked at her best friend. As usual, Naomi looked stunning. Hair and make-up perfectly applied, and wearing yet another brand-new, matching Nike gym outfit, with the whitest Nike trainers on the market. Even the girls on the reception desk were looking at her admiringly.

'Sorry,' Suzie replied. 'I've got a problem, and I'm not sure what I should do about it. Do you fancy a coffee first so that I can go through it with you?'

'Of course,' Naomi replied. 'I'll order a couple of cafetières, and we can go to that lovely room at the back overlooking the golf course. No one else will be there at this time of the day.'

Naomi went over to the desk and placed her order. She was

intrigued, as she had never seen Suzie in this mood before. They found a seat in the corner, a table with the most wonderful views. The coffees were placed on the table, and then the member of staff left them in peace.

'I can't believe what has happened,' Suzie started, voice trembling. 'Stevie has said he wants a divorce and wants to move away and take the twins with him!'

'What?' Naomi said, sounding shocked.

Suzie then described Stevie's plans in detail. Her version was slightly different from the truth, as it made her sound like the perfect mother. It was also interspersed with a few fake tears. At the end of the rant, Suzie burst into tears – real ones this time – although she wasn't sure whether these were for the situation or for her future in general.

'What we need to do is make sure that you come out of this okay. I can't cope with losing my best friend,' Naomi said after Suzie had managed to control her sobs a little. 'Don't worry about the house. I can easily talk Freddie into letting you stay there. He has plenty of properties anyway. What we do have to do, though, is make sure Stevie comes out as the bad half of the relationship so that you get as much as possible. Do you remember Gloria Wilson? She used a solicitor called Annabel something or other who specialises in grabbing blokes by the balls in divorce proceedings. Poor old Hamish, her husband, ended up living in a bedsit on his own.' She appeared to be warming to the idea.

Suzie sat listening, liking what she was hearing.

'I'll get her number off Gloria, and I'll come with you to see her if you like?' Naomi said.

'Sounds like a good idea to me,' replied Suzie, drying her eyes on a napkin.

'There must be a whole host of things we can blame on Stevie. The fact that he is never there can add to his neglect of you and the twins,' Naomi continued. She was enjoying this now. 'I know you have never mentioned it, but surely you must wonder what he's up to on all of his trips away. A good-looking guy like Stevie, and he has the gift of the gab. Freddie has always said that Stevie is the smoothest-talking salesman he has ever met.'

Suzie thought for a moment before replying, 'It had crossed my mind, as I know what he's like, but I never thought he would be unfaithful to me.'

'Don't kid yourself, lady. All men have the potential to be unfaithful. That's why I never let my Freddie go too far out of my sight!' Naomi said, laughing.

'I've just remembered something odd,' Suzie suddenly thought out loud. 'I was looking though his wallet last night and found a receipt tucked away in it.'

'What for?'

'It's for two suitcases in the left luggage department at Victoria station. I can't understand what he was doing there. He didn't mention that it was a place he was visiting this week.'

Naomi laughed. 'Of course he wouldn't mention it. He's not likely to tell you where he was taking his fancy piece, is he?' she said, staring at Suzie as if she were a child. 'Come on, Suzie, you need to switch on. There's no use believing what he has told you. He's obviously up to something. You don't suddenly want a divorce for no reason.'

'I never really thought of it like that, although it did come out of the blue. We've had our problems in the past, but I thought everything was fine now.'

'Right, there's only one thing for it,' said Naomi, standing up.

'What?'

'Me and you are going on a road trip!'

'Where to?' Suzie replied, looking puzzled.

'To London to collect those suitcases,' Naomi stated earnestly. 'It may be our only chance to catch him out. He has obviously covered his tracks well in the past, as you've never noticed anything. But the fact that he has a receipt for something he has not mentioned before is suspicious in my mind. You know he is with the twins all day today, so he can't collect it. Maybe he was planning on getting them tomorrow instead, in which case it would be too late. This is our only chance, and the journey from Nottingham to London is less than two hours, so we can get down there and back without him knowing. We can even have a bottle of Prosecco on the train each way to celebrate!' Naomi began laughing.

Suzie was already warming to the idea. After this morning's realisation she hadn't really fancied a spa day today, and the fact that she could combine a couple of hours' quaffing Prosecco with finding some dirt on Stevie added to the attraction. She smiled at Naomi for the first time that morning.

'Let's go!' she said, giving her a high five, before they both burst into giggles and marched out of the spa.

CHAPTER FORTY-THREE

Clare had made another coffee and finally tracked down a car for her and DS Sellings to use. Not an easy feat in the current climate. All the cuts to budgets meant that there were now half the number of vehicles that there had been a couple of years ago.

The number crunchers had worked out that vehicles weren't being used enough and that they could cope with fewer. That was great when looking at the figures whilst sitting in the ivory towers of headquarters but didn't work out on the ground. What couldn't be accounted for were days like today, when one of the cars was off the road due to a minor accident, one was in for servicing, two were being used to visit inmates in prison and two more were already booked out on jobs that morning, leaving Clare with the remaining one, which was also booked an hour later. Luckily it would only take fifteen minutes to go and get Jackson and bring him back, so she promised that it would be returned in time, and she and Bill got on their way to the Foyer.

Whilst en route, she filled him in on the comments that Emily had made about Jackson in general.

'I'm starting to not like this guy before I've even met him,' Bill said.

'Don't worry, you wouldn't do anyway. There's something about him that rings too many alarm bells,' Clare replied. 'And before you say anything, it's not just a woman thing. I've met enough creeps and weirdos over the years to know.'

Bill laughed. 'And made them cry!'

'Not you as well! I've already had Simon Crofts throw that at me this morning!' Clare said with pretend exasperation.

'You know you love it. And what were you talking to him about?'

'Just sounding him out about the potentials of this job.'

Bill smiled to himself. He knew Clare would have done; he trusted her fully. He just wished he had more DCs like her.

Having arrived at the Foyer, they were able to walk straight in, as the front door had been left propped open by a fire extinguisher. This was against fire regulations but something that happened a lot, with tenants just nipping out for a cigarette all the time.

Clare and Bill walked right up to the office, where Ronnie was engrossed on his computer.

'Morning, Mr Jackson!' Clare boomed with slightly too much gusto.

Ronnie jumped at the intrusion on his thoughts, but quickly hid his shock when he saw who was talking. Clare was experienced enough to spot the moment of panic, even though he recovered fast.

He cleared his throat and replied with a feeble 'Good morning. How can I help you?'

'Just following up on the missing girl, Bethany. This here is my detective sergeant, Bill Sellings. As we have had no trace of her, the enquiry is becoming more serious.'

'So, you haven't heard from her at all? What about her

phone?' Ronnie asked, not liking the way the DS was looking at him.

'It has been turned off for some time and was last used not far from here, so that adds to the intrigue,' Clare said. 'I have reviewed the case with my colleague here, and we have decided that as you knew Bethany well, we would like you to come to the police station to give us a statement.'

'I didn't know her that well, only as I was a manager here.'

'I realise that, but she appears to have very few friends, and so, at this time, you probably knew her better than most of the others. It's a voluntary visit so that we can get as much information as we possibly can in statement form. It's so much better than trying to do that here,' Clare said, not letting Ronnie have time to answer.

He didn't really like the idea but also knew that if he refused they may read something into it, and he didn't want that to happen.

'Yes, of course. I just need to get someone to cover my duties here. I won't be a minute,' he replied as helpfully as he could before calling Josie and explaining the situation. Luckily, she was just finishing in a meeting on the other side of the building and was able to get there within a couple of minutes. Ronnie handed everything over to her in his normal, methodical way.

'How long will you be gone?' she asked.

Ronnie shrugged and nodded towards the two detectives.

'I'm sure it won't be too long,' Clare said, smiling, and she saw Ronnie relax a little. 'Just want to get as much information about Bethany as we can. The girl's been missing a while now. Are we ready then, Mr Jackson?'

'Yes, let's go,' replied Ronnie, not feeling as enthusiastic as he had sounded, and still not liking the way the DS was looking at him.

CHAPTER FORTY-FOUR

The bottle of Prosecco on the train from Nottingham had made Suzie feel a lot better. The shock of Stevie's announcement and the hangover had finally cleared. She was glad Naomi had made the decision she had, as Suzie wasn't sure what she would have done otherwise.

Naomi had become her most trusted friend over the last couple of years. It helped that she had an unending source of money and was happy to pay for anything and everything. Whenever Suzie questioned this, she was always given the same answer: 'Freddie loves treating me.' Suzie knew that before she had met up with Naomi, the poor girl had been bored – just a trophy wife to a man who was a workaholic. Suzie's arrival on the scene had not only given her a new lease of life but also a friend who could enjoy that life with her. Suzie also knew, from the times when she had met up with Freddie, that he loved the fact that Naomi and Suzie were such good friends and he was happy to foot the bills.

They settled into the journey, and the discussion turned to the suitcases and what to do with them. They were obviously part of the secret life that Stevie had been living and would give them clues as to who he was seeing. The first question was where to take them to look in them. Naomi had come up with another great idea. The Clermont was a four-star hotel and part of Victoria station. She went online and booked a room and lunch there. The idea was to take the cases to the room, find evidence of Stevie's misdemeanours, and then head down to the restaurant to celebrate with lunch and a bottle of bubbly, although this time it wouldn't be the cheap stuff: a bottle of champagne was on the agenda.

After they got off at St Pancras station, Naomi hailed a black cab to take them to Victoria. There was no way they were going down into that awful Underground system, especially as they were both a little tiddly. The driver was a typical London cabbie, a chatty type who couldn't understand why they burst into fits of laughter when he asked them what the trip to Victoria was for.

Eventually Naomi managed to compose herself enough to reply, 'We are going to find out if my friend Suzie here is going to get a divorce or not.' This made them both giggle again and ensured that the cabbie gave up on them. He appeared to have decided he would rather wait and see if the next customers were a bit more sensible.

When they arrived at Victoria the girls thanked him and gave him a fiver tip, so he didn't think them so bad after all. Both needed the loo so they tottered down the stairs before checking out where the left luggage department was.

The Latvian lad on the desk gave the girls a big smile, liking what he saw: two attractive ladies who were obviously happy about something. Suzie handed over the receipt, and his colleague went off to collect the two cases. He tried his chat-up lines on them but realised from the way that they looked at him that the lines wouldn't work on these two. They didn't seem to work on many women in the UK. Maybe it was time to revamp his technique, he thought as he handed over the two cases.

Suzie and Naomi grabbed the cases and started walking over to the entrance of the hotel in the corner of the station.

'These look like new cases,' remarked Suzie.

'Even more reason for suspicion. If he wasn't up to something, he would have used some of your own cases,' Naomi replied and gave her a triumphant look. She was enjoying this now and was ready to help her best friend get through this ordeal. If it all worked out, she would have more time with Suzie, something that pleased her.

Since Suzie had had the twins, Naomi had seen less and less of her. If Stevie wanted to take them away, it would mean more fun for the two of them.

They entered the hotel and were welcomed by a polite young Eastern European receptionist.

'Blimey, aren't there any English people working down here?' Naomi remarked a little too loudly.

Suzie giggled again. The receptionist chose to ignore the remark and carried on professionally, explaining the room location and the details for lunch.

Naomi thanked her and ordered a bottle of champagne to be sent to the room.

The two of them made their way to the lift. The elevator glided up to the third floor, and they stepped out into the corridor. As often happens when staying in a hotel, they had that moment of slight confusion as to which direction the room was in, but they eventually managed to find it.

The bellboy arrived with the cases at the same time as the champagne in an ice bucket with a few canapés on the side from room service. Naomi thanked them, giving each a tip, before pouring Suzie and herself a glass.

'Here's to your future, whatever it brings!' she said, clinking glasses with Suzie.

'Let's get these cases opened. Do you want me to do it?' Naomi asked.

'Yes, please,' replied Suzie, this was the moment she had been dreading.

Naomi clicked the locks on the first case. Nothing happened.

'Shit, they're locked,' she moaned.

'We should have thought of that,' said Suzie. 'What are we going to do now?'

'I know,' shouted Naomi. 'I've got a nail file in my handbag. We can force those pathetic locks easily.'

Again, Suzie was glad of Naomi's quick thinking. Her friend had certainly been a star today.

Naomi fished the nail file out. It was a strong one about four inches long. She put it under the catch and twisted, and the lock gave way.

'Aha, that was easy,' she said, attacking the second catch and popping that one too.

The lid came open, and all she could see were bin liners and tape. Suzie had turned her back, not wanting to look, but when she heard the disappointed 'Oh' from her friend, she spun round.

'What on earth is in there?' she asked.

'Don't know, but my trusty nail file is about to find out,' Naomi answered as she tore into the black plastic. The nail file did the job.

That was when the screams started.

CHAPTER FORTY-FIVE

The short trip back to the patrol centre was very quiet. Clare and Bill wanted it like that to make Jackson feel even more uncomfortable. Both the seasoned detectives might have normally chatted to their witness in this situation, but neither of them wanted him to relax. They both knew that this was the last situation that Jackson wanted to be in, but at the same time he couldn't really say no.

He was here to help.

Once they arrived at the centre and had been buzzed in the front door by the front desk assistant, the three of them entered a hive of activity and the detectives attempted to find a quiet room to take the statement. This wasn't easy, as it was handover time, and so there were even more staff than usual milling around.

Jackson had never seen so many police officers, PCSOs and support staff in his life and found it all a little intimidating but tried not to show it.

Even though the building was open plan, there were a few 'quiet rooms' in the central area. These were for private meetings, either between managers and staff or to talk over a case, and could also be used for taking witness statements. These rooms would never be used for suspect interviews, which had to be formally recorded and held in official interview rooms.

The only problem with these rooms was that they were built in glass-walled compartments, which wasn't the best planning idea. They were soundproofed, but everyone could see in. Any interview, including a good old-fashioned rollicking, or something emotional and personal, which may end in tears, was completely on view.

The truth was that most people in the building were too busy concentrating on their own work to worry about what was going on in any of those particular rooms, but the occupiers always felt that people were watching them, whatever the situation.

Unsurprisingly, Clare had managed to obtain one of these rooms, again to make Jackson feel uncomfortable. There were other more private rooms available – quieter and out of the public view – but she wanted Jackson to feel he was on show.

Clare made them all coffee, and they began the witness statement. Bill took the lead, asking Jackson to describe his job and how long he had been there, before moving on to the present case.

'So, how long have you known the missing girl, Bethany?' he asked.

'Since she arrived about a year ago,' he answered.

'How well do you know her?' Bill continued. He let Jackson know that he was talking about her in the present, making sure not to intimate that anything had happened to her.

'Not that well. In fact, I don't think anyone knows her too well. She certainly keeps herself to herself.'

'So everyone keeps saying,' Clare said. 'But as one of the managers at the centre, you would have been able to read about her background, wouldn't you?'

'Well, yes, I could, but apart from a general look on their arrival, I don't try to delve too deep, unless it becomes necessary. I prefer to take them as they are and hopefully help them in the present and in the future. It's not good to dwell on the past.'

'Indeed,' replied Clare, and left the response hanging in the air for a little bit longer than was required. 'However, you do know the timings of her movements to and from the Foyer, don't you?'

'Yes, but that's only because she is such a good worker and is always on time, unlike a lot of the guests we have. The fact that she is one of the first out each morning soon becomes obvious, even to new staff.'

'What about coming in from work? What time is that normally?' Clare probed.

'I wouldn't notice that as much, as I don't often do the late shift. There are always willing volunteers for that shift, as it suits certain people to work later in the day, whereas I like to be in nice and early and have the evenings free. But I know she usually catches a bus from Pevensey Bay just before ten which normally gets her back home by eleven.'

'Okay,' continued Clare, 'so on the last day Bethany was seen, you saw her leave that morning.'

'Yes, I did. I was showing a new manager, Josie, around and Bethany walked through the reception area. I introduced them to each other. We had a quick chat about The Moorings, as Josie likes it out there.'

'So, were you still around when she should have returned?' Bill cut in.

'No, I finished around seven thirty and went home.'

'Can anyone vouch for that?' Bill asked.

'Sorry, what?' said a flustered Jackson.

'Can anyone else vouch for you that you were at home that evening?'

205

'Well, no, not really, as I live on my own. Why would that matter?'

Clare took over. 'We need to know to eliminate you from our enquiries. You see, we know Bethany went to work that day, and we know she was there until around ten, when she left for the bus. But nothing was heard from her after that, although her phone record shows that she did return to Eastbourne that night.' Clare left a long enough gap to let the information sink in, then continued: 'We have checked with the bus company, Stagecoach, and they have said that the last bus was cancelled that evening, as the original one broke down in Bexhill, and they were unable to get a replacement on the road at short notice. We have also checked with all of the local taxi companies, and none of them picked her up that night. So she must have got from Pevensey Bay into Eastbourne either by walking, which I very much doubt at that time of night, or by getting a lift from someone. From what I have gleaned about her so far, I can't imagine her hitching a lift, so the only other possibility is from someone she knew.

'We've spoken to all those who worked at The Moorings that night, and none of them saw her after she left or gave her a lift. So it must have been someone else that she knows, and, as you said, she doesn't know many people, so the ones she does know are our only lines of enquiry at this moment in time.'

There was a pause, which felt like a long time to Jackson as he looked at both detectives, not really knowing what to say. Both looked back at him with quizzical expressions, so that he knew he had to say something.

'I know nothing about that, and I wouldn't have been out driving at that time of night,' he replied, trying to take the tremor out of his voice.

'That's fine,' replied Clare, 'but you need to be able to prove you weren't, and so far, you haven't been able to do that. You say you were at home. Can anyone corroborate that? A neighbour or friend perhaps?'

Jackson felt trapped even though nothing was being said accusingly.

'I doubt it. All of my neighbours are elderly, their curtains are closed by six, and all are deaf as posts. I just stayed in and watched TV and went on the computer for the evening. Nothing out of the ordinary.'

Bill seized the chance a split second before Clare could. 'How about your computer? Is there anything on there that could prove you were indoors and using it that evening? We can get our experts to have a quick look and help prove it for you.'

Jackson went red and stared at the floor.

CHAPTER FORTY-SIX

Anna, the Latvian chambermaid, heard it first.

The scream was like nothing she had experienced before. She knew it was serious so ran straight to the room it was coming from and knocked on the door. The screaming continued, although there was no reply to her knock, so she rapped again, asking if everything was all right.

No reply, but she could still hear the woman in the room so made the decision to open the door with her master key.

She saw two women. One was screaming and the other was being sick in the bin. She looked on the bed. There was a suitcase with black bags inside, but as she got closer, Anna could also see some blood.

She called security on her walkie-talkie, saying it was an emergency. Thomas, the head of security, was there within a minute. He had heard the tremor in Anna's voice and some sort of screaming in the background and guessed straight away something was wrong. As he entered the room, he wasn't sure who to go to first, as Anna was crying, one of the guests was screaming, and the other was retching into the bin. He went to the suitcase on the bed and saw blood and flesh.

Thomas dialled 999 and asked for the police. He then led the three women to the next room and let them sit down in there. He knew the police would want to see them but thought it would be better if this happened out of view of the case and its contents.

He heard the sound of the patrol car's sirens from a few streets away. He checked out of the window and watched two officers park the car in the drop-off area outside the hotel and run into the building. A short time later the officers arrived at the floor. After asking Thomas who he was and what had happened, they accompanied him into the room. It only took them a matter of seconds to look into the case and see what everyone else had.

'Right, everyone out, and we'll call for SOCO,' the first officer said. He was quite short for a police officer, but very stocky, and obviously a bodybuilder.

'We can start a scene log outside the room and leave everything as it is. It makes it so much easier for the SOCO team,' he explained to Thomas.

His taller, thinner colleague was already on the radio asking for them.

'Let's go into the other room and let's hear what everyone else has to say,' the first officer continued.

Thomas opened the door to the next room, and the two officers walked in. The three women had calmed down a little. Suzie had finally stopped retching, Naomi was now only sobbing, and Anna was just sitting staring at the wall.

'Does anyone want to tell me what happened?' the shorter officer asked in a soothing but serious way.

He saw the two guests look at each other and the older one nod to the younger one to make her tell the story.

'My friend thought her husband was having an affair, and we found a left luggage receipt in his wallet for Victoria. So we decided to come and collect it to see what we could find out about the affair. We've just opened one of the cases, and there's blood and what looks like flesh in there, whatever it is. It stinks like nothing I have ever smelt,' Naomi blurted out without taking a breath.

'I must admit it doesn't smell too good, does it?' the kind constable said. 'We have our forensics team on their way. They deal with all of that kind of stuff. All I need you to do is tell us what happened fully, so that we can write a statement. I also need you to tell me the name and whereabouts of your friend's husband. It looks like he needs to answer some questions.'

CHAPTER FORTY-SEVEN

Jimmy Shadbolt had been a SOCO for two years, but he hadn't attended many major crimes. This was because he worked for British Transport Police, or BTP as it was commonly known. He had attended the same national training centre as all the other SOCOs from around the country, but on return to his force, his role would be different from that of his course-mates. BTP only had jurisdiction on crimes that happened on railway property, which meant that most of the time he was working in railway stations, investigating burglaries and thefts.

It meant a lot of travelling, as the force only had a small number of examiners, since not many were needed on a daily basis. The BTP SOCOs came into their own when there were any major train disasters, as that was their main remit.

Some of his colleagues had worked on the Hatfield and Potters Bar crashes and would tell stories of their involvement. Jimmy listened in awe because there hadn't been anything like that since he had been in the job. He secretly wished there would be soon, despite it meaning that there may be people who lost their lives. That was one of the negatives of being a SOCO. You couldn't do the best parts of the job until someone died.

Today, though, Jimmy had taken a call which sounded as though it could be something interesting. He had been in the BTP HQ, which was right next to Victoria station, when he got the call. All he had been told was that body parts had been found in a suitcase in one of the rooms of the nearby hotel.

Jimmy was intrigued. He ran through possible scenarios in his mind as he approached the building, but since it was something he hadn't dealt with before, he wasn't sure what to think.

The concierge spotted him straight away, recognising Jimmy from when he had been there a fortnight before when one of the rooms had been broken into, and so he approached him.

'Would you like to follow me, sir?' the small, immaculate man asked.

Jimmy was glad. It saved him the awkwardness of trying to explain to a receptionist while guests were around. He followed the smartly dressed man into the lift and along the corridor to the officer who was scene-guarding the room. After a quick introduction to each other, and a wait for the concierge to get back into the lift, Jimmy asked, 'What have we got then?'

The officer told him all he knew, which wasn't much. How security had called them, how the three traumatised women had been found in the room with a suitcase on the bed which had been opened slightly and appeared to have some blood and body parts inside, and 'Oh by the way, it smells of decomposing flesh.'

'Thanks for that,' replied Jimmy with a grin, although not smiling inside.

'A couple of other things I noticed before we got them out of the room,' the officer continued. 'There's another matching suitcase on the floor, and there is also a pile of vomit in and around the bin, which belongs to one of the women we found in there.'

'The day's got even better!' said Jimmy, grimacing as he started to climb into his PPE.

'So, any idea of the story?' Jimmy asked.

'It appears that one of the women suspected her husband was "over the side" with someone, found a left luggage receipt for the station, recovered the cases and brought them up here to look through and find proof of his infidelities. They had even bought a bottle of bubbly to celebrate with!'

'I can't believe that!' Jimmy answered with a real smile this time.

He finished getting dressed, checked the time with the scene guard and had his name added to the scene log, then he photographed and opened the door to the room. Jimmy stood at the doorway and photographed the room from there. Once that was done, he grabbed his equipment and closed the door behind him.

Now he was alone in the room with whatever else was in there. He felt a little strange. He was usually told exactly what would be in a scene by the attending officers, who had normally had a look themselves and found whatever he had been called to investigate. This time was different. He had no idea what to expect.

As he walked around the room, taking photographs from all four corners and other general shots, he could hear his heart pounding. It was so quiet in the room that he could hear all the sounds from the street outside: the engines and horns of cars and buses, and the normal sounds of people going about their daily lives unaware that up here he was about to discover something gruesome.

Lots of those people would sit and watch horror films and scary programmes on the TV, completely oblivious to what real dead bodies looked or smelt like. Jimmy could smell it already. Although he was fairly inexperienced, he had come across the acrid odour of decomposition several times, and it was something he could never forget.

He began taking photographs of the suitcase on the bed. It was heavily bloodstained, and he could see the flesh the others had reported. As soon as he opened the black plastic, there was no doubt in his mind that it was definitely human remains. He could see part of a face – only an eye and some hair, but that was enough. Jimmy carried on photographing as much as he could but decided he wasn't going to go much further whilst in the hotel room. There was only one place to look at all this properly, and that was in a mortuary, with clean, sterile surfaces, good lighting and a pathologist.

Jimmy wasn't going to try to guess what body parts he had in there. Having completed the photography of that suitcase, he forced open the other one and looked inside, taking photographs as he went. He could see that the contents were similar but didn't cut through the plastic to find out what was inside. It was obviously the same, and he was happy to let the examination continue under controlled conditions.

Jimmy packaged both cases in polythene bags, sealing them securely, before placing them in large brown paper sacks. He then called his supervisor, Callum McIntyre, to tell him about the job. Callum was pleased with what he had done so far and said he would arrange the mortuary and pathologist, and also for undertakers to attend. Callum knew that mortuaries wouldn't accept any body parts such as these unless they were brought in officially. It might be just a part of the scene to the SOCOs, but it was someone's dead body and needed to be handled with respect.

Jimmy went outside and let the scene guard know what was happening. For now the officers would stay there, as the room needed to be kept sealed until after the examination of the suitcases at the mortuary.

CHAPTER FORTY-EIGHT

In the interview room, it had all gone quiet. Clare and Bill didn't say anything. Neither needed to. Jackson's complete change in demeanour meant that their earlier suspicions were right. He didn't want to let them see his computer to find out what he had been looking at the night before. The truth was there were no grounds to do that at this stage, but the intimation that he should give it in voluntarily was a trick to see his reaction, and it had worked.

Jackson was mad with himself. He knew that most of the decent stuff on his computer was heavily encrypted and probably wouldn't be found with a basic quick search, but it didn't matter. He didn't trust the police, especially not these two. If he handed over his computer to try to prove he had been on it the night in question, he guessed they would use some type of scanning software that might pick up something from his hidden world. Jackson was also furious with himself for giving off obvious signs of embarrassment. He couldn't control them.

'Is there a problem with that?' Clare said, enjoying every second of his squirming.

'No, not really. I didn't think you would need to go that far to check someone's alibi,' he mumbled.

'It was your fault. You said that no one else could vouch for you and your whereabouts, so this would make things easier,' she answered in a professional tone.

'I thought I was here to write a witness statement to help find Bethany, and now you're treating me like a criminal.'

'Of course you aren't,' soothed Bill. 'It's just that you know more than most about Bethany and her life and her normal movements. As she's gone missing, you're the best person to talk to. The fact that you can't tell us what you did the night in question leaves us with a gap in our enquiries that we would like to fill in. There's also the fact that you have, in the past, been questioned by the police with regards to your interest in youngsters. You can see how it looks to us, can't you, Mr Jackson?'

Jackson let out an involuntary gasp. 'What do you mean? I have never been charged for anything by the police.'

'You weren't charged for anything precisely, but you were questioned several times,' Clare took over. 'We all know that times have changed and a lot of the stuff that people got away with in those days wouldn't be ignored nowadays. I have spent many years dealing with "non-offenders" from twenty years ago, and most were lucky they got away with so much. That's all I am saying.' She stared at Jackson.

'I don't like what you are insinuating,' Jackson spat. 'I have no police record, I came here to help with your enquiries, and you are trying to twist things around to suit your investigation. I demand that you let me leave.'

'Of course you can leave, Mr Jackson,' Bill stepped in. 'You are under no obligation to stay at this time. We just have to cover all avenues. You have been very helpful to us, and I'd like to thank you for attending,' he said earnestly, although Jackson seemed to catch the element of sarcasm in his voice.

Everyone stood up, Jackson unable to make eye contact with Clare, who was staring at him for effect.

Jackson couldn't get out of there quick enough. Clare arranged for a PCSO to give him a lift home and again thanked him for his help before seeing him to the door.

'What do you think?' Clare asked as soon as he was out of view.

'I'm not sure either way, but I do know he doesn't want us to look on his computer!' Bill replied, laughing.

'I know. I wish that was being recorded. That would have been a perfect one for training school!' She grinned. 'I thought he was going to collapse in front of us!'

'True, but we maybe need to do a bit more digging into his history before we can arrest him and bring him in. So far, it's just coincidental that he knew the victim. Without his background, we wouldn't have looked twice at him.'

'I know that too, but there's something I don't trust about him. And I'm going to get to the bottom of it. At this time he's our only suspect.'

'I shall leave it up to you to find out anything else you can about our friend Mr Jackson then,' said Bill. 'After you've made the coffees, that is!'

CHAPTER FORTY-NINE

Stevie was having a great day. After the shock of what Suzie had said to him, he had strapped the twins into the car and driven off, glad to be away from her. The twins were smiling and waving to him in the back seat every time he checked on them. He loved every minute of this and couldn't understand why Suzie didn't. Stevie knew he wanted to spend more time with them, and his new plans would enable that.

He only had to drive a few miles before arriving at Sherwood Pines. This was an area of Sherwood Forest that was used for all types of outdoor pursuits. There were miles of walks, cycle tracks, even a tree-climbing area.

There were also plenty of paths through the woodland, which eventually led to an area where there were log cabins to stay in in the middle of the woods, complete with all the mod cons, including an outside Jacuzzi. Stevie and Suzie had stayed in one once. Suzie had enjoyed sipping bubbly whilst sitting in the Jacuzzi but had to leave after the first night, as she had been kept awake all night thinking she could hear strange scratching noises underneath the lodge. It wasn't really her type of break.

Stevie smiled at the memory; it just about summed her up.

After he had parked the car and made sure the twins had their wellies on, the three of them went exploring into the woods. The two little ones loved it, running through puddles, whooping with joy. They would suddenly stop when one of them found something new on the ground, looking at Stevie for advice. Stevie would then explain to them what that particular leaf or cone was, and they would listen for a second before running off looking for the next exciting find. This was what being a parent was about, Stevie thought, and his new job meant he would have more times like this.

By lunchtime, he could tell they were tired. Stevie bought them each a snack box from the café and grabbed himself a sausage roll. They were struggling to stay awake, so he took them back to the car and settled them into their car seats. Both were asleep within seconds. Stevie checked his phone. There was no signal in the forest. For a split second he almost panicked – modern-day life meant he always needed to be online for one reason or another – then he relaxed and laughed to himself for being like that. Here he was, cut off from the world in the middle of some woods, with the twins asleep and nothing else to worry about.

He sat in the front seat and closed his eyes and even nodded off, until one of the twins murmured, meaning that both would be awake within a minute. Stevie let them out of their seats and they headed back to the woods. He had spotted an area where other children had made dens and took them there. For the next hour or so, it was time to make the Johnson camp, all three enjoying the experience immensely.

Having completed their task, they wandered back to the car. Stevie said he had a surprise for them and took them back into the café. He secured them in a couple of high chairs and went over to the counter and returned with hot chocolate drinks topped with cream and baby marshmallows. The twins nearly burst with excitement, and the three of them shared the sickly-sweet treat together. Once they had finished, Stevie used nearly a whole pack of wet wipes on them. After which they drove home in the car.

He had just parked on the drive when a police car pulled up behind him. Two officers got out.

'Mr Stevie Johnson?' asked the female officer, an athletic-looking young woman with blonde hair.

'Yes?' Stevie answered.

'We need to speak to you, sir.'

'What about?'

'I'd rather we went inside and discussed it.'

Stevie explained that he had the twins in the back, both of whom had dropped off to sleep on the journey home.

'That's okay, sir. Get them settled and we will come in then,' the male officer replied. He was older than his colleague, with greying hair. He had an attitude that said he had seen it all before, and he was already looking at his onboard computer for their next task.

Stevie went into the house, his mind spinning, not really knowing what to think except that he had to compose himself. He took the twins to the nursery and settled them in their beds. He then walked back downstairs and invited the officers into the kitchen.

'Sir, we have been asked by another force to help them with their enquiries,' the female officer said.

'Go on,' replied Stevie.

'It appears your wife is in London and is claiming she found a receipt for left luggage at Victoria station in your wallet. Do you know anything about that?'

'No, I don't!' replied Stevie. 'And I don't know what she's doing in London, either. She's meant to be at a spa for the day.'

'Right, so you don't know anything about the receipt or the cases?' the male officer asked.

Stevie thought quickly. 'No, but what I do know is that we argued yesterday, and I suggested that maybe we would be better apart. I know she's not happy about it, so this might be something she made up to get at me. Anyhow, I haven't even been to London for ages, probably a year. I spent the beginning of the week in Sussex and Kent. Any other time I was here.'

The two officers exchanged glances. It appeared both had already made their decision.

'That's fine, sir,' the female officer said. 'Sorry to bother you. As I said, we are just following up enquiries from another force. It's the Met Police, who do tend to get excited about certain things!' She smiled and left.

The male officer was already getting back into the car, obviously more interested in some of the real work that was awaiting them rather than a wild-goose chase from the Met.

Stevie closed the front door and let out a deep breath. He hadn't been as clever as he had thought. Why had he kept that receipt? It wasn't as if he was ever going to use it.

CHAPTER FIFTY

The Royal London Hospital was in busy Whitechapel, an area that showed the full diversity of the city, with a hectic street market in the road opposite, and nose-to-tail traffic at all times. The mortuary was similar to those in most hospitals – not signposted and hidden from view. If he hadn't been there before, Callum McIntyre knew he wouldn't have been able to find it. He could tell that Jimmy, in the passenger seat, was nervous, as he hadn't stopped chattering since leaving the base.

Jimmy was telling Callum about the women in the hotel and how it had been a strange experience for him. The CID officers had viewed the footage of the women collecting the suitcases from left luggage and their arrival in the hotel and had all agreed that the women's demeanour led them to believe their story. There was no way they had been expecting to find what was in those cases. The officers had taken statements from both women and then they had let them go. Officers from Nottinghamshire Police had been requested to speak to the husband.

Callum and Jimmy parked outside the mortuary and rang the bell. After a while, the door was opened by a short chap with a beard who introduced himself as Adrian and motioned for them to follow him. The two SOCOs looked at each other with raised eyebrows. Mortuary assistants were quite often a little odd, and this one seemed to fit the bill.

They changed into PPE and went into the PM room, where the two suitcases, still packaged in brown bags, were on the mortuary slab. Adrian appeared almost from nowhere to tell them that Andrew Eaton, the pathologist, had just arrived, and that he would be ready in a few minutes.

Jimmy prepared his camera and started photographing the cases. Eaton had already been briefed by the time he walked in, and having checked that the photos had been taken, he set to work on the packaging of the first case.

Once it was all cleared and the pathologist had removed the lid, Jimmy took photographs of the five individually packaged items, including the one that had been slightly opened. The stench of decaying flesh hit them straight away, even making the pathologist pull a face.

He finished opening that package and found it was a right arm. As well as photographing it, Jimmy and Callum also took some fibre tapings and swabs for DNA. This process was then continued as they separately unpacked the other arm, two legs and a head.

'Appears to be the head of a young adult female,' Eaton announced to the others.

'Can you give us a better description for the enquiry team?' Callum asked.

'I would guess that these are brown eyes, although now slightly discoloured, and her hair looks dark brown, although there appears to be dye added,' Eaton said. 'She looks petite, and I will guess that the other suitcase contains the torso, so shall we have a look at that then?'

Adrian and Jimmy cleared another slab and prepared the package for him. After more photographs, Eaton opened the case to find exactly what he had expected. After a good look over the torso, he told them there were no further distinguishing marks on the body for identification purposes, so they would have to use either DNA, fingerprints or dental records.

Eaton then placed all the body parts together to make a full human form on the mortuary slab. He roughly measured the height of the body and then carried out a full post-mortem, recovering as many of the samples as possible.

At this stage of the post-mortem, it was impossible to tell what might have happened to a person before their death, so every possible sample was needed. The only remark Eaton made was that all the cuts on the body were clean, meaning a very sharp knife had been used. *Not really much use in this particular case*, thought Callum.

He had already contacted the local traffic police to see if they could get a motorcyclist to run some samples up to the forensic lab in Abingdon, Oxfordshire. The inspector in charge had given him the normal answer, that traffic police weren't there to be used as a courier service, but after Callum explained the seriousness of the case and the need for an answer as soon as possible, the inspector relented and said he would get someone over as soon as possible.

Callum knew from experience that even though that was the official stance on these types of requests, the traffic officers loved the chance to get out on the motorway and open up their BMW bikes for a change. He wondered what speeds they really hit on these runs, as no one would be checking them. The bikers always seemed pleased with themselves anyway.

There was a knock on the door. He opened it and a motorcyclist was standing there waiting. Callum gave him the DNA swabs from the limbs, which he had placed in a small freezer box with an ice block. These boxes were produced for picnics and for taking sandwiches to work. Callum always wondered whether the manufacturers realised what else the containers were used for. He gave the leather-clad cop the details of the scientist he had spoken to, who would be staying late so that she could get the sample prepared that night. It would then be put through the system and be ready for the morning. This was the premium service that the lab offered. It cost quite a lot of money – over two thousand pounds – but was worth it for police forces, as it could lead to a case being solved quickly, saving time and money. Callum knew that if the lab was able to get a DNA hit the following day this mystery would be solved sooner.

By the time he had finished with the traffic cop and returned to the PM room, Andrew Eaton had finished and was washing his hands.

'Nothing else of note to tell you,' Eaton said blandly. 'No form of ID in the cases or on the body so far. It will be up to you to identify her, and then we can take it from there with regards to what has happened.'

Callum thanked him and Adrian for their assistance and then helped Jimmy take his equipment and samples out to the van.

Once inside the van, Jimmy asked, 'What do think?'

Callum replied, 'Could be anything or anyone at this moment in time.'

Jimmy looked disappointed, so Callum continued: 'Depending on what the DNA result is tomorrow, we might have some more work to do.'

'I hope so!' replied Jimmy. 'I could do with a decent job.'

CHAPTER FIFTY-ONE

Naomi had taken charge again once the police had left. Suzie was still in a daze, so Naomi made the decision that the two of them would book another hotel and stay the night. She called a taxi and told the driver to take them to the Savoy. She and Freddie had had lunch there the year before, and the food had been excellent, so she knew it would be a great place to stay – firstly, because of the luxury, and secondly, to try to get over what had happened that day.

Once they had checked in and ordered a bottle of the finest champagne on room service, it was time to try to get Suzie back into the real world. It had been a strange twenty-four hours for her. First, Stevie turning up early, then announcing he was leaving with the twins, and then the discovery of the cases and their contents. Naomi balked a little as she remembered what was in those cases. Even though she had only seen a little bit, it would stay with her forever.

'How you feeling now, love?' she asked tentatively whilst handing Suzie a glass of bubbly.

Suzie's far-distant gaze remained in place. She still appeared to be in shock. Naomi sensed she may need more time so went and sat on the chaise longue in front of the window.

'Bastard!' Suzie said.

Naomi was shocked, as she had never heard Suzie speak like that before.

Suzie seemed to have come around from her trance. She continued, 'Bastard, bastard, bastard!'

Naomi didn't really know what to say.

'I knew we'd not been seeing eye to eye for some time, I knew he wasn't happy with me, but why did he do that? Do you think he was trying to frame me? Do you think he did all that on purpose, knowing I would find that receipt and then making it look like I killed someone so that I would get locked up and he could have the twins? Do you think that's what he planned?'

Naomi hadn't really thought of it like that, but she had wondered how it was all connected. Suzie's interpretation seemed to fill almost all the holes in the story, and she enjoyed the idea.

'That explains it. Stevie was having an affair and wanted to leave you and have the twins but guessed that you wouldn't give them up voluntarily. So he got someone to kill a woman and leave the body in London for you to find, knowing that you would get the blame, as you are the estranged wife and he could make out that you did it, to give you a bad name so that you wouldn't get custody of the twins.'

Both stared at each other for a moment as those thoughts sunk in.

'So now we know what he was up to and that he has failed, there's only one thing to do,' said Suzie.

'What?'

'We need to celebrate. We need to celebrate that bastard's failed plot, and we need to celebrate my freedom. Here's to us!' Suzie exclaimed, clinking her glass against Naomi's.

Naomi was just glad that Suzie appeared to have got over it all and was now back to her normal self.

'We can finish this and then have something to eat in the Savoy Grill,' Naomi said. 'It's the most wonderful restaurant I have ever been to. We can then go out and party. We can celebrate your freedom, and we can celebrate that conniving toad of a soon-to-be ex-husband of yours, who is now hopefully going to prison!'

Suzie cheered, and they clinked glasses again.

This was going to be a night to remember.

CHAPTER FIFTY-TWO

C allum had only been in the office for half an hour when the phone rang. It was an outside line, which was unusual in his office, so he guessed it might be the lab. It was, and after the normal pleasantries, the scientist got down to business.

'I have a DNA match from one of the samples you sent us yesterday,' she stated formally. 'It is a female called Bethany Brooks, aged eighteen.'

'Thanks for that,' replied Callum. 'Do you have any other information?'

'I can tell you that she had her DNA taken five years ago, aged thirteen, for an alleged assault and has not been in custody since, so you were really lucky that she was on the National DNA Database. In fact, nowadays with the new rules, she probably wouldn't have been still on there.'

'Wow, that was lucky,' Callum answered. 'I'll get on to our intel department and see if we can find out where she is from. Thanks ever so much for your prompt work.'

'That's okay,' said the scientist. 'It's a shame we can't report all submissions this quickly. but we've just got such a volume of work at the moment that we're only prioritising special cases like this. I've also just emailed you the result.'

Callum thanked her again and put down the phone. He opened his email account and read the summary. So, the poor victim he had watched being taken out of those cases yesterday now had a name: Bethany Brooks.

Callum wondered if they would ever find out the truth of what had happened to her. He printed off the email and went down the corridor to the intel section. He could have just sent the email on to them, but he wanted to follow this up personally. He had a strange feeling of sympathy for the victim and wanted to make sure that this enquiry was dealt with as quickly as possible.

Callum walked into the BTP intelligence section, and the first thing he heard was a deep voice saying, 'Blimey, there's a sight you don't see very often: a SOCO!'

He looked over to where the voice had come from and saw Rod Underwood, an older ex-detective who had been around forever.

Before Callum could even say hello, Rod continued with his banter: 'What's the matter, Callum? Is it too damp out there for you? Have you managed to actually find a fingerprint this year?'

There were giggles from around the room as other officers warmed to the entertainment. Callum, having heard all the lines many times before, just replied with, 'Is that you, Rod? I thought you would have retired by now. Is your eyesight good enough for you to see that computer?'

Rod threw his head back and laughed. He liked a bit of a joke, something he felt was missing from the job nowadays. He was just about to continue ribbing Callum when his supervisor looked up from her screen to see what all the commotion was. Rod noted it and then motioned with his eyes to Callum, who instantly realised what was going on.

'I've just got a DNA match to a body we found yesterday, and I wanted to know if you could do a trace of the name for me.'

'Of course I can. Give it here,' Rod replied professionally, giving Callum a slight wink before changing screens from what he was doing before. The truth was, Rod was pleased to get involved in something decent for a change. Being an ex-detective, he missed this type of work. Most of what he did these days was just inputting intelligence into the system, and he was bored with that.

It didn't help that Rod didn't really get on well with his young female civilian supervisor either. That probably had something to do with the boring work he was given.

He typed the name into the system, including Bethany's date of birth. All that showed up at first was the information that was already known – that she had been questioned about an alleged assault five years before.

'Looks like your victim has been a good little girl since then,' boomed Rod.

Callum spotted the wince from the supervisor in the corner. *Poor Rod. He's becoming a dinosaur, and he's the only one who hasn't noticed*, thought Callum.

'Let me try a few more systems,' Rod continued, completely unaware of what was happening around him.

He tapped away, swearing twice as his sausage-like fingers managed to hit keys he didn't want them to. The supervisor was not only wincing now, she was sighing. Callum wondered whether he should have just sent an email.

'Bingo! I've only gone and found her!' Rod shouted excitedly, punching the air and looking triumphantly at his supervisor, who wasn't watching. 'She was reported as a misper two days ago, down in Sussex.'

'So, what is she doing ending up in a suitcase in Victoria?' Callum said out loud.

'That's for some real detectives to find out,' said Rod with a hint of disappointment, knowing that it wouldn't be him anymore. 'I've got a contact name here for the officer in charge of the investigation if you want?'

Callum nodded, pen ready.

'It's a DC Clare Perks. That would be WDC in my day, but I know none of them want to be called that anymore, and her number is as follows ...'

Callum noted the number, as well as yet another sigh from the supervisor at Rod's latest inappropriate comment. He felt sorry for Rod. He was obviously struggling in today's modern police force, but he had come up trumps when needed. Callum thanked him and said his goodbyes before heading back along the corridor to his office. He now had a phone call to make, and the outcome of it would decide whether he would continue to work on this job. He very much hoped he would.

CHAPTER FIFTY-THREE

Clare Perks had spent two hours in the CID area trying to trace further evidence about Ronnie Jackson. She was getting more and more frustrated. Every time she found associates of his and the possibility of a better crime line, the trail disappeared.

Clare decided it was time for a cigarette and went outside to the smoking area. She was chatting to a couple of the admin staff when her mobile phone rang. She looked at the screen and saw 'Private Caller' and pressed the green button to answer, stating her name formally.

'Hello, DC Perks. My name is Callum McIntyre. I'm a senior SOCO in BTP.'

'How can I help you?' Clare replied.

'It's not how you can help me, it's how I can help you,' Callum said. 'We have found the body of someone you have reported as a misper.'

'Who?' answered Clare, not wanting to tempt fate.

'Bethany Brooks.'

'Where was she found?' Clare asked, her mind spinning with so many other questions.

'She was found cut up in two suitcases in left luggage at Victoria station.'

'Oh no!' was all Clare could say at first. 'Any idea how she got there?'

'No. CCTV has been checked and an image recovered, but it's a bloke wearing a baseball cap and sunglasses, so not much to go on.' He then ran through the story so far, leaving Clare standing open-mouthed and the other smokers wondering what was happening, as it wasn't often anyone saw Clare Perks speechless.

Callum finished the tale and then asked, 'Do you think this will stay with BTP, or will you hand it over to your officers?' He knew what the answer would be already. Sussex would want to take this over. It annoyed him because it happened on a lot of the jobs that started on BTP property.

Clare said she would need to speak to her superiors first and let them make the decision. She also asked Callum to send her an image of the offender by email. It might not be good enough for a positive ID, but it might be enough to rule Jackson in or out of the enquiry. She also asked him to email the images taken in the hotel room and at the mortuary, then thanked him and said she would be in touch.

Clare went straight into Bill's office and told him the news.

'The first thing we need to do is get on to the major crime team and get hold of an SIO,' he said, scrolling through his contacts. 'I know Tom Mead was on call at the beginning of the week, as he was dealing with Op Dundee. Let's hope he's still on. I'd rather have him than one of those Surrey ones. All of them think too highly of themselves.'

He phoned Mead and asked him if he was still on call. Tom replied with a cautious affirmative.

'I have a real whodunnit for you!' Bill replied.

'Oh yes?' answered Mead, intrigued. 'I think you had better come over and tell me about it then.'

'We're on our way,' replied Bill as he and Clare headed to the door to walk over to the next building, where the major crime teams were housed.

'Can I–?' started Clare.

'Of course you can,' said Bill with a cheery smile. He knew that the first thing she would ask would be if she could stay on the job. As usual when these situations occurred, he was short-staffed, but he would never stop a member of his team from working on a major crime. He also knew Clare would enhance the enquiry team.

CHAPTER FIFTY-FOUR

Tom Mead was indeed still on call. Although to be truthful, he was looking forward to having the weekend off, especially having worked long hours at the beginning of the week on Op Dundee.

However, when he received a call from someone as experienced as Bill Sellings saying that he had a 'real' job, Mead knew it would be something good. He called Alison Williams and told her to come to his office as well. He didn't have to wait long for them all to arrive. He heard Bill's and Clare's excited voices coming along the corridor. Everyone said their quick hellos, and then Mead suggested coffee.

Clare looked at the two men and rolled her eyes. 'How do you like it, guv?' she asked.

'NATO standard please,' he replied. 'If you're up for making one for Alison, she's on her way, and she'll have a Julie Andrews.'

Clare had not heard that one before and looked questioningly back.

'It's white with none. Do you get it? A white nun?'

Clare groaned and made her way to the kitchen, Tom and Bill's laughter echoing down the corridor.

Alison arrived just as Clare returned with the drinks. All sat down, and Clare started telling the story of the enquiry so far, the two senior detectives taking notes as she spoke. Tom was impressed with the level of investigation that Clare had already carried out. He knew she would want to be on the enquiry and was secretly glad that she would be.

It took Clare almost half an hour to cover all the facts, and at the end of her report the room fell silent as everyone took stock of what she had just told them.

Mead broke the silence. 'You were right, Bill. This is certainly a Cat-A murder. We don't get many of those.'

'I know,' replied Bill. 'We have Jackson as a suspect at the moment, but evidence of his involvement is only circumstantial. If he has an alibi, or if we have a look at the footage from the station and decide it's not him, we have no idea who the offender is.' He looked at Clare.

'We also have no idea what the motive is,' said Clare. 'It appears that Bethany was a very private individual who kept herself to herself. Bless her, she hadn't had the best of lives, mainly in care, and didn't deserve to end up like this. I'm just thankful she had her DNA taken for an alleged assault at one of the children's homes when she was younger, or we wouldn't have a clue who she was.'

'Anyway,' said Mead, 'I'm taking the decision that we will run this as a major crime, and MCT will take the lead.'

'Just a quick one on that: the BTP senior SOCO who did the scene and the PM asked if they would be needed,' said Clare.

'As it stands, we will be using our own SOCO staff. There's no need for them at this stage, plus I don't think our own Mr Crofts would be too impressed if we gave this one away!'

'I think he'd already guessed that. I'll let him know.'

'Right then,' said Mead. 'I'll organise a briefing at one o'clock if you, Alison, can get as many staff together as possible.'

'Friday afternoon briefing. Just think of the moans,' Bill joked.

'I know, but for every moaner, there's always someone who will relish the overtime,' Tom replied. 'Can you get the images ready for the briefing?' he asked Clare.

'I shall get on to Simon Crofts,' Clare said. 'I'm sure he'll sort it out. I did have a quick word with him about this job a couple of days ago, although he won't know about the finding of the body yet.'

'Good. See you all at one in the conference room,' said Mead as he and Alison went to start the policy book, the most vital part of an SIO's paperwork. It would describe how the investigation would proceed, and the thinking behind all the decisions he would make over the coming days.

CHAPTER FIFTY-FIVE

The conference room was buzzing as Crofts entered. Word had obviously got around, and everyone was looking forward to working on a real job for a change. It was a fairly spacious room, with a large centre table and seating for around thirty people, with extra chairs if needed. At one end were big screens with the Sussex Police logo. These were used for making TV appeals for information, usually when someone had gone missing.

Crofts quickly greeted one or two of the detectives he knew, but his priority was to get the computer and screen working so he could show the images to everyone at the briefing. He had spent the hour since his call from Clare downloading the images taken by BTP into his account and preparing them for showing. The room was also used for general meetings and training, so the computer system was still set up the way the last people who had used the room had left it, which meant it wasn't ready for what Crofts would require.

Luckily, he had been through this routine many times, so he soon had the right cables plugged in and was ready for when the presentation was needed. More and more staff were arriving in the room. The usual banter between old friends, and between different departments, was in full flow. *Even more than usual,* Crofts thought. It was like an end-of-term assembly; the nervous energy pumping around the room was almost making people giddy with excitement.

The chairs were all full, except for three at the top of the table for the management group. There were even some staff standing at the back, all carrying the pale-blue official investigator's notebooks that everyone used for taking down details.

The door opened, and in walked SIO Tom Mead, Alison Williams, and Kevin Bates, who would be the DS in charge of the incident room. A hush fell and everyone took their seats.

Mead started by welcoming everybody and informing them that the enquiry was to be known as Op Arrowhead. He then explained that not everyone in the room would know each other, so everyone attending should introduce themselves to the team. Mead started, followed by Alison and Kevin. Crofts was next, and then, individually, people gave their names and roles all the way round the room. There was a mixture of detectives from MCT and from division, there were MCB analysts, an exhibit officer, a disclosure officer, even typists from MCB. Everyone ready to go. Mead then went through the briefing from the start, including everything known so far.

When the time came to show the images, Crofts began with a warning that some of them would be upsetting. This was something that he never would have said in his early days, as everyone had been expected to deal with things like that, but nowadays it was standard. Crofts could tell from their reaction to the images that people were shocked. Looking round the room, he could see expressions of horror, disgust and even nausea, as well as a few who seemed genuinely interested in what a human body looked like once it had been chopped up. It wasn't something that many of them would have seen before.

Tom Mead then asked Clare Perks to give an update on how the investigation was going. Clare told them about Ronnie Jackson and his background, and how he had reacted when asked about his computer. There were knowing looks across the table. Clare said she had viewed the CCTV footage from Victoria station and was pretty sure it wasn't Jackson.

'He is much larger built than the suspect on the video. It doesn't mean that he wasn't involved, it just means that he didn't take the suitcases to the station,' she finished, and sat down.

Mead then asked if anyone else had any knowledge of the job. There was no response, so he continued: 'As you can see, this is a real Cat-A murder enquiry. We have a body that went missing in Eastbourne but then turns up in London. The only suspect so far appears to have been ruled out of some, if not all, of the enquiry. We now have to follow several lines of enquiry. We need to look into Bethany's background as much as possible to see if there is any reason someone wanted her dead. We need to look into the CCTV systems at Victoria and try to trace the man with the baseball cap and glasses from left luggage back into the station and back to where he arrived from. We also need to look into the luggage: where can it be bought from and how old is it? And we need to investigate the husband of the finder of the body, Stevie Johnson. The wife says she got the receipt from him. Local plod has been to see him, but he denies all knowledge – but he would, wouldn't he? I understand that he is a sales rep, so we need to find out where he has been recently.'

He let the orders sink in before saying, 'Just because I am an SIO, doesn't mean I can think of everything. Does anyone else have any ideas?'

Everyone looked around at each other, but no one spoke.

'Okay then, Kev will start handing out actions based on what we are asking at this stage. I want them started straight away, and then a further briefing at 1800 tonight. Good luck, everybody,' Mead finished. He then left the room, followed by his deputies.

Crofts closed the computer system and headed up the stairs to the SIO's office. He knocked on the door. Mead looked up and beckoned him in.

'Thought I'd just have a quick chat about the forensic strategy and any other forensic needs,' Crofts said.

'Thanks for that,' Mead replied, and then the two of them sat down and went through everything dealt with so far. Each of the scenes had been given a designated number, which both men had agreed on. As far as they could see, there was nothing else for them to add, as it had all been covered by the BTP SOCOs.

'What I will do is write a strategy covering all of that, and then add details of any further scenes. I would imagine we will have a murder scene somewhere at some stage, so I will include that,' said Crofts.

Mead thanked Crofts and turned his mind to the hundreds of other tasks that would now occupy his day.

CHAPTER FIFTY-SIX

Crofts didn't have to wait until the briefing at six o'clock to get an update. He got a phone call from one of the MCT detectives, Martin Buller.

'We've got a potential scene for you,' he said excitedly.

'Blimey, that was quick,' said Crofts, genuinely surprised.

'You can always count on MCT. You know that, Crofty.'

'Are you going to tell me or just gloat all day?' Crofts said sarcastically.

'It's probably easier if you come up here and we'll go through it.'

Crofts put down the phone and left his desk to find three SOCOs looking at him expectantly. 'Do you lot ever miss anything?' he asked with a smile.

'That's what we're paid for!' Leighton Phillips answered with a grin. 'Is there anything you want us to do?'

'Don't go anywhere at the moment – tell the desk that I said so. We might have some work to do later,' he replied, and then he made his way out of the office and headed up the stairs to the major incident room.

Buller was on the phone as Crofts entered the outside

enquiry team office. He motioned for Crofts to sit as he continued his conversation.

'Yes, guv, I have Mr Crofts with me now. I'll let him know. Thanks, sir.'

He put the phone down and looked at Crofts.

'It's okay, I'm just organising the scene guard for you. If I do any more to help you, I might as well do the scene myself,' he said, laughing.

Crofts shook his head but smiled. 'That's all I need: incompetent scene examination!'

'Touché!' replied Buller.

'So, what have you got?'

'Do you remember the husband of the woman that found the remains?'

'Stevie something.'

'Yes, Stevie Johnson. Did a quick background check on him. Seems he works for Pfizer, the pharmaceutical company. So, I phoned their head office to see what he was doing last week.' He looked at Crofts, who was giving him his full attention. 'Luckily, he had been in to their HQ this week for a meeting. Whilst there, he had updated all his expenses claims, including some from the Sussex area.'

'Go on,' said Crofts.

'He was in the Eastbourne area the night Bethany went missing, and – you won't believe this – but he stayed in the Travelodge on the seafront that night. One phone call to the hotel, and it was confirmed that a Mr Johnson did stay there that night, in room twenty-eight. Of course, when booking it, he wouldn't have been trying to hide his identity.'

'That's lucky!'

'It's not luck. It's called good detective work,' Buller said.

'If you say so,' Crofts replied, although he was impressed by how quickly Buller had found the information. 'Do we know if the room has been used since?'

'I'm afraid it has. Johnson checked out Tuesday, and it was cleaned that day. It was used Wednesday night and then cleaned again. So at least it's not dirty!' Buller joked.

'That doesn't help us on the forensic side of things though,' Crofts responded dejectedly.

'I'm sure a man of your calibre will find something,' Buller replied, before adding, 'We're just checking through CCTV in reception to see if we can find the victim with him, which will save you the hassle of trying to prove it forensically.'

'Even if you get it on camera, that will only put her in the reception area with him. Any good defence lawyer would be able to talk their way out of that one. We need to put her forensically in that room. Thanks anyway. Can you let the SIO know that I will write a strategy for him, and we'll head down to the scene?'

'Of course, but the local inspector isn't happy. She's hardly got enough staff as it is, and now she's having to cover that all night – on a Friday night as well.'

'It's tough at the top, isn't it?' said Crofts. 'It looks like my Friday night is ruined too.'

They smiled at each other, and Crofts made his way back down to the SOCO office.

As he walked in the door, he was greeted again by three eager faces.

'Right, I need two of you for a scene that will need to be finished overnight. Who's up for it?'

Three hands went up. Crofts smiled. SOCOs loved murder scenes. People from other walks of life might find that a little strange, but for them it was an opportunity to use their considerable skills – and it didn't happen very often.

'Okay, I'll take Hannah and Leighton, as you're both on

tomorrow. Ellen, you're into rest days tomorrow, so it's better if you miss out for now. I'm sure there'll be others,' he added, seeing how disappointed Ellen looked. He always tried to be as fair as possible, but he couldn't please everyone all the time. 'If you can get yourselves and your kit ready, I've just got to compose a strategy, and then I'll give you a briefing.'

Two happy members of his staff went to prepare themselves, while the other gloomily returned to the statement she was writing.

CHAPTER FIFTY-SEVEN

S uzie was drunk. She knew she was drunk but wanted to get even more drunk. She wasn't sure what she would have done without Naomi. They had consumed more bubbly and then headed to the Savoy Grill. The food was, as Naomi had said, excellent.

Their starters were fish goujons, with medallions of steak in a sauce for their main course, followed by fruit and coffee. It was all needed, not only to fill them up but also to sober them up a little. During the meal there had been plenty of talk, but neither of them mentioned the events of that morning, which suited them both.

After their meal, they had decided it was time for more bubbles, so drank a bottle at the restaurant and then ventured out and had found a great wine bar with live music. This was the place for them.

The bar was very busy. Whilst Naomi went to the toilet, and to the bar on the way back, Suzie kept going over what had happened in her mind. How could her husband have done that? Was he really trying to frame her to get rid of her? What made him think of that idea? Did

Stevie really hate her that much? What was going to happen now?

Suzie knew she could never see Stevie again. She thought she had been unhappy with her life with him as it was, but this had completely changed everything.

She was brought back to her senses by the return of her friend, who was just as drunk as she was. Naomi tottered up with two more glasses of bubbly and two young men in tow.

'This is Suzie, and this is Brad and Josh,' she slurred.

Suzie smiled at the two drunk young men, who were obviously City workers of some kind and were very good-looking, but she wasn't really thinking about meeting someone new at this moment in time. Brad already had an arm around Naomi, and she could see Josh was angling to sit next to her.

'I'm sorry, Naomi, but I need to go home now. I feel sick,' Suzie said.

She saw Josh jump back away from her and give Brad a look that said he was getting away from this one.

Brad looked disappointedly at Naomi, but she wasn't looking at him, just worriedly at her friend.

'Okay, let's go!' she just about managed to slur.

'Am I coming too?' Brad asked.

'I don't think so. I'm a married woman!' Naomi replied.

'Since when has that been a problem?' Brad asked.

'Since my wedding day, you cheeky bastard,' Naomi responded defiantly.

'You shouldn't chat us up then, prick-teaser,' Brad replied.

'I didn't chat you up. You did the talking. Now bugger off before I call security,' Naomi shouted, managing to get the attention of several people on the next table.

'Okay, okay,' said Josh, grabbing his friend and moving away. 'Let's get away from this pair of bunny boilers!'

'Cheeky sod!' said Naomi, grabbing an empty champagne

bottle by the neck, ready to use it on the young men, who were backing away.

Security had actually already turned up and saw Naomi with the bottle. Luckily, due to her drunken state, she didn't have a very strong hold of it, so one of the burly doormen took it from her while he escorted her towards the door, politely but firmly. Suzie retrieved their handbags and followed, silently glad they were being asked to leave. She had really had enough.

As they got to the door, where the doormen were already ordering a cab for them, she heard Naomi say, 'You wouldn't be doing this if you knew what happened to us today!'

The doorman, professional as ever, answered, 'I'm sure I wouldn't, madam,' as he beckoned a cab over to them. 'Where are you going?' he asked.

'The Savoy,' Suzie answered.

The doorman looked genuinely surprised. It wasn't an address two drunken women would usually ask for. He opened the black cab door, told the driver where the women were going and helped them both into the back seat. He closed the door and mouthed a silent 'Good luck!' to the driver, who just shook his head and then drove off. It was obviously just a normal night for him.

CHAPTER FIFTY-EIGHT

Crofts had spent half an hour finishing the forensic strategy for the scene in room twenty-eight. It was a simple one really: everything in that room needed forensicating.

Everything would need to be photographed, every surface fingerprinted. They would be swabbing for DNA material absolutely everywhere and taking samples of every area of the room. They had to find a trace of the victim somewhere in that room, even though it had been cleaned twice and also been slept in since the suspect had been there. A swab with a minute trace of her saliva or blood or any other body fluid. A fingerprint or even a hair; any of those small items could potentially give them their answer.

The other samples might also be needed later if Bethany's clothing was found; it might even be a case of matching fibres. The team would recover everything and go through it with a fine-tooth comb, as the saying goes. Never was it more apt than when working on scenes like this. Crofts actually liked this type of examination better, as it was a challenge.

Many of the murder scenes he dealt with were just a case of

recovering items for the sake of it. Everything in a job like this could be potentially important, and he loved it.

Hannah and Leighton listened intently to his briefing and then had a quick chat about everything that they would need to do.

'Don't forget the toolbox,' Crofts said as they prepared to go.

'What?' Hannah asked.

'The toolbox,' Leighton replied for Crofts. 'We'll probably be taking the sink and shower apart, won't we?'

'But it's been cleaned twice and used since,' replied Hannah.

'Never say never,' said Crofts. 'We'll take it all. Travelodge will need to order a new everything once we've finished.'

The three of them gave a little cheer and walked out to their vans.

The drive to the seafront hotel only took a few minutes. They got out and headed into the building with all their kit and were met by Martin Buller in the foyer.

'I've got some good news and some bad news,' he said.

'Go on then. Give us your worst,' Crofts replied.

'We've checked through the hotel CCTV,' Buller said, motioning to the discs in exhibit bags he was holding. 'We've got a full face on Johnson arriving on Monday afternoon, and we've also got the same with him going out for the evening later the same day. However, we have no other traces of him later that night or the next day.'

'Why not?' asked Leighton on behalf of all of them.

'Even though this system has a good, clear picture, unlike some, it also uses several cameras, and the recording flits from one to the other repeatedly. Lots of CCTV systems are like this, mainly used for general security only. They just cover overall views, and then if anything interesting comes up the operator will home in on it, but it only records the particular areas it's focused on. If the suspect happens to walk in or out when the cameras are looking at other areas, the cameras may not catch him. It is just random really, but our suspect got lucky on this one.'

'So that means we have no record of the victim being at this hotel either,' Crofts said.

'Or that she has ever been in the hotel,' added Hannah.

'That's right, folks. No pressure then,' Buller replied with a grimace.

The three SOCOs looked at each other with disappointment.

Crofts then cut through any negative thoughts. 'It doesn't change anything for us. We will still be carrying out the same examination whether there is CCTV or not. As with all major crimes, there are lots of parts to the jigsaw. The forensic part is the most important for us, and we will recover everything we can from that room. The results of that may or may not be needed to complete that jigsaw. We just get on and do our job properly and let the others in the enquiry do theirs.'

'Hurrah!' said Buller, impressed with the pep talk, having felt a little down himself on seeing the images.

'By the way,' Crofts said to the other two. 'I hope you realise it's going to be a long night.'

CHAPTER FIFTY-NINE

The room was the same as many in this type of premises. Not the largest of areas, but with enough space for a couple staying for a short period of time. The bathroom was off to one side – again, not the biggest available, but one that fit in with the shape of the original building.

Hannah had gone in first, photographing as she went. As usual the four quarters, before homing in on any items she deemed as relevant. She had first photographed any slight stains on walls and on the carpet. Leighton and Crofts had then started testing areas for blood, but none were coming up with a positive reading so far.

The room had been cleaned twice, so the housekeeping staff would have removed any obvious marks. These rooms were used daily, and the staff knew how to prepare them for the next guests without leaving any trace of previous occupants.

In the bathroom, the sink and the shower tray were swabbed. But the results were still negative for blood. Having swabbed all areas for DNA, they then started to work on the sink U-bend. It meant cutting through the plastic pipe and carefully removing the bend itself. They then decanted the water from it into a tin, as that would also need testing once it got to the lab. The U-bend was then packaged separately. They didn't swab it there, as they had decided to let the lab have a go at that under sterile conditions. Next it was the trap from the shower tray. This wasn't easy. Whoever had put this in had used plenty of mastic, probably to avoid leaks, but it meant that Crofts and Leighton had to cut an even bigger hole than usual to get to the trap.

Sussex Police would pay for any damage caused by the SOCOs. In the past they had recovered whole doors, window frames, carpets, settees and mattresses from major scenes. If there was evidence to be found, those items were needed.

After about half an hour of sawing, twisting and swearing, the trap was finally removed, and again they decanted the liquid into a tin and then packaged the rest separately. They then stripped the bed and packaged the mattress in a large sack made specifically for that purpose. The sheets had been changed twice since the event, but any fluids from the night in question could have seeped onto that mattress. There was no way of knowing at this stage what could be found, so it was better to take the whole thing.

Having finished with that task, they continued to swab and fingerprint every surface in the room. Nothing at this stage was coming up as an obvious piece of evidence, but everything possible was recovered. Once the exhibits were examined at the lab, they might yield some DNA material that wasn't obvious to the human eye.

All areas of carpet, the bedding and the chairs were then fibre-taped by the team. This was in case they had to place either the victim or the suspect in the scene using those fibres against clothing recovered at any time during the enquiry.

There was a knock at the door; it was Martin Buller with some coffees. Crofts told them to have a break, and the three of them disrobed and went and sat in one of the spare rooms to drink and stretch.

'How long are you lot going to be in there?' Buller asked. 'Haven't you got homes to go to? It's nearly three o'clock, you know.'

Crofts just smiled. He knew his old friend had only really come along to get an update on what had been found, but he didn't mind. The caffeine injection was most welcome at this hour.

'If you must know, we haven't found anything relevant so far,' admitted Crofts. 'We've recovered loads of exhibits, so hopefully the lab will come up with something good at a later date.'

'That's a shame. I could do with something more for the interviews. He's just "no commenting" at the moment, thanks to his solicitor. Although we do have quite a lot of circumstantial evidence, any little piece of forensic evidence will always help.'

'That final piece of the puzzle, hey, Crofty?' Leighton replied with a smile, as it was one of Crofts' favourite sayings.

It made him smile too. At least his team were still happy at this time of night. He wasn't sure how much sleep they would all get, and he was looking forward to the BBQ that afternoon. It wouldn't be the first event in his private life he had had to cancel, and it wouldn't be the last. He mentally worked out how much longer it would take at the scene and how much sleep he may get and decided he should be able to make it.

Buller left, and the team replaced their PPE and went back into the scene.

'Right, it's the final push. Let's finish off this swabbing and powdering, and then we can go home,' Crofts announced, and the three of them set to work.

It was another hour before they were done. That was when

Crofts said to the other two, 'We're just about finished, except for one thing.'

Both looked at him quizzically.

'The bed,' Crofts said. 'We haven't moved it or looked underneath it.'

He saw the look that passed between them, but also knew they were both too tired to argue. He and Leighton grabbed one side of the bed and stood it on its side against the wall.

'Gross!' said Hannah.

Crofts turned and looked. Although the room was generally clean, as it would be in any hotel, those standards hadn't included checking under the bed. It looked as if it hadn't been moved for some time, Crofts guessed. As well as a thin layer of fluff, there were old tissues, some of them soiled, and even false nails, toenails and a comb. All of which would now need to be recovered, packaged and exhibited.

'Sorry,' said Crofts as they set to work. 'It had to be done.'

'Yes, we know,' replied Leighton, this time without humour, as he started recovering the items.

Crofts got his torch out and had a look around the underside of the bed. What he spotted made him swear.

'What's up?' Leighton and Hannah asked in unison.

'Come and look at this,' said Crofts excitedly.

Leighton and Hannah both examined the area he was illuminating with his torch. It was a stain; only a small smear, but it looked like blood.

Hannah took some photos, and Leighton prepared the blood-testing kit. He folded the small testing paper into quarters and rubbed it over the stain lightly so as not to remove it all. He then took the test paper over to his case and applied the chemicals. If it was blood, it would turn purple.

It did.

The three of them shouted 'Yes!' at the same time, and

Leighton added a 'Whoop whoop!' as they high-fived each other.

This was followed by a concerned voice outside asking, 'Are you all right in there?'

It was the scene guard on the landing, who hadn't heard a peep from them all night but had come to investigate the sounds of celebration in the room.

'We're okay,' replied Crofts. 'In fact, we're feeling better than we have all night,' he added.

The scene guard shook his head and muttered to himself that he would never understand those SOCO people.

CHAPTER SIXTY

SIX MONTHS LATER

Stevie Johnson sat back and thought about the journey he was on. He was heading down to Sussex to stay, just as he had wanted.

Unfortunately, he wasn't going to choose where he lived, and his twins wouldn't be with him. The journey was towards a cell in Lewes Prison.

It had all happened so quickly and had all gone so wrong.

It felt like one minute ago Stevie had been enjoying his time with the twins, made even better by the fact that Suzie hadn't returned to their home. He had taken this as a positive. She had obviously realised what he had wanted for them all was the right answer, after all. He had enjoyed a few full-on days with just the three of them before the police had arrived and arrested him. Stevie still couldn't remember why he had thought he had got away with it in the first place. Surely, he should have realised when the first coppers had visited him that he would be a suspect.

All he could think of was that he must have pushed it to the back of his mind and carried on, oblivious to it all.

Why?

Maybe he had known he would be caught and had been enjoying as much time with the twins as possible.

Who knew?

Stevie had also had plenty of time to think back to what had happened from the minute he had met Bethany. He had lots of 'if only' thoughts.

If only the bus had been on time, he wouldn't have given her a lift.

If only he hadn't taken her for a drink.

If only she hadn't got drunk.

If only he hadn't taken her to his room.

Why hadn't he just arranged for her to get home?

Even then he hadn't set out to do anything to her. It was all a sequence of events that could have been avoided.

If only.

The arrest was bad enough as it was, but it was made worse when he'd asked about who would look after the children whilst he was in custody. The police officer looked at him strangely and just replied, 'Their mum'. As Stevie was about to argue and tell the officer about how bad a mother Suzie was, he spotted her over the officer's shoulder. He looked pleadingly at her. She just stared back at him with a face full of venom and hatred, a look that he would never forget.

Stevie was then led out to a car and driven down to Sussex to be interviewed.

At the start of the interview, he decided he would just deny it all and stick with the story that Suzie was trying to frame him. However, that all changed within the first half hour of the interview.

His solicitor sat him down and gave him a quick briefing, saying that he should go 'no comment' to start with to find out what evidence there was. Stevie was happy with that.

It started with what seemed a pleasant chat. They asked

him about himself and his job, all of which he talked about freely. Even when they asked about his trip to Sussex, he was happy to answer their questions, as he knew his movements might have been tracked through his work arrangements.

It was when they started to ask questions about Bethany that he decided to begin the 'no comment' tactic.

However, what the interviewers told him started to change the story. Not only had his car been tracked by automatic number plate recognition throughout that afternoon, they also knew that he had stopped at The Moorings, because of the receipts and from witness statements. One of those witnesses also reported him laughing and joking with Bethany.

The ANPR also tracked him back into Eastbourne at the time Bethany was trying to get home. There was also CCTV from the Crown and Anchor of them both in the pub, as well as witness statements putting them together in there.

Stevie thought he would maybe be able to say that, yes, he had been with her, but then said goodbye to her and went back to the hotel room on his own. However, that idea was crushed when he was asked if he had taken Bethany to the room.

'No comment,' he replied.

The interviewing detective then paused before saying, 'We may have evidence that can put Bethany in that room.'

Stevie didn't say anything but just looked at his solicitor, who, sensing a problem, asked for a recess. Once alone, Stevie asked the solicitor what he should do.

'I would suggest that at this stage you continue to go "no comment". If you try to challenge anything, it will only make things worse.'

So Stevie did.

Once back in the interview room, he'd been asked about the body, about the suitcases, about the journey to Victoria, and the left luggage, all of which he'd no commented. He'd carried this on for the rest of the interviews over the following forty-eight hours, wondering what would happen next.

Stevie had soon found out. The interviewing officer had come in on the third day and told him that the CPS had agreed that he should be charged with murder and had agreed to keep him in custody. Within an hour he was on a bus to the remand wing at Lewes Prison, which was not a nice place.

His solicitor came to see him a month later and told him of the updates he had been given.

In room twenty-eight, over 120 exhibits had been recovered. Traces of Bethany's blood were found to be in both the sink U-bend and the shower trap.

It had taken Crofts and his team ten hours to complete the scene, and an hour of that was just getting those two items removed, but it was worth it.

The investigators had also found a smear of blood on the underside of the bed. That small mark had probably been from when Stevie had loaded the body parts into the bin bags and must have slightly touched the underside of the bed. It didn't matter; it was enough to get a full DNA profile, meaning that it could be proven that Bethany had been in that hotel room.

Other test results came from the bin liners used in the suitcases. Stevie's fingerprints were found, using superglue treatment, on the bin liners. This was probably from when he'd bought them in the shop. There were also lots of glove marks from when he had been using gloves in the room, but it was those earlier fingerprints that proved it was him.

There was also saliva on one of the ends of the masking tape. This was probably from when he had torn a piece of tape off with his teeth when he was packaging. One bite left enough DNA on the tape to give a full profile.

Away from the forensic side of things, the investigation had also tracked him on CCTV that day from the left luggage area, pulling the suitcases back onto the platform, on the train (where he took his sunglasses off), back to Eastbourne station, and then back through the town centre.

The CCTV systems used throughout this journey were many and varied. Some were systems in the streets and some were from shops along the route. It didn't matter where the footage was from; his whole trip had been recorded.

He had even been caught throwing the clothing and phone into the bin in the town centre. The enquiry team had contacted the refuse company, and a search team had gone out to the landfill site where it had been deposited. The supervisor had been able to tell the search team exactly where that bin had been emptied. The team had dug down until they found newspapers and receipts from the correct times and then searched through the rubbish in that area.

The searchers even found the clothing, which they could prove through testing for her DNA had belonged to Bethany. They also found her phone and, in the dying light at the end of the last day, the SIM card and battery for that phone.

At the end of the explanation the solicitor just sat and stared at Stevie.

Stevie didn't know what to say, so asked a feeble 'What happens now?'

The solicitor thought for a while and then told him there was so much evidence against him that it wasn't worth even trying to go for a 'not guilty' plea. Stevie didn't argue with this.

He suggested that Stevie pleaded guilty to manslaughter, saying Bethany had been a willing visitor to the room, had bumped her head, and then he had panicked and not known what to do so had disposed of the body to hopefully get away with it. That way, his admission and the manslaughter plea would mean he would receive a lesser sentence.

Stevie knew he was beaten and agreed.

The trial was brought forward due to the guilty plea. It didn't take long, and at the end of it the judge, in his summing up, thanked Stevie for his admission and said he had taken that into consideration. However, whatever had happened to an innocent young girl in that hotel room had then led to Stevie carrying out evil deeds, and so the judge had no option but to hand out the longest sentence available to him for manslaughter, and that was a life sentence.

Stevie's head drooped as the reality of it sunk in.

He heard a whispered 'Yes!' from somewhere in the gallery but couldn't make out who had said it. He did, however, notice Suzie sitting there. He hadn't noticed her before and didn't know how long she had been there. The look his wife gave him was one of triumph, and Stevie had to look away.

He had heard that Suzie was now a perfect doting mother to the twins. The whole episode had changed her completely, and she had told her friends that all she wanted in life was to be a good mum to those poor children, who would have to grow up knowing their father had killed someone. This had upset him even more. Seeing her now looking down on him after the sentencing twisted the dagger already in his heart.

He would probably never see her or them ever again.

The 'Yes!' had actually come from DC Martin Buller. The detective hadn't meant it to come out so loud. He had been to many trials over the years and was used to getting good results so didn't know why he'd said it.

Buller hadn't realised it, but this job had meant a lot to him. The main reason was that he had often been to The Moorings and had recognised Bethany from the first pictures he had seen of her. Indeed, she was the same age as his daughter, Danielle. He had found the original problems with the CCTV recordings and knew that it would be a hard task for Crofts and his team when he had left them that night. He knew that the SOCOs had stayed there all night, but boy, did they get the results.

He had also been at the interviews when Johnson had tried to avoid commenting, even though the evidence was stacked against him. He had spent his career as a detective listening to 'no comment' interviews. He knew the reasons behind this procedure but hated the fact that many criminals hid behind it, sometimes even smiling through their interviews, knowing there was that protection. Buller was relieved to see one of those criminals finally be charged. There was only one thing more for him to do.

He headed for the police witness room in the court, which was now empty, as the trial was over. He scrolled through his phone contacts and pressed the green button. It rang for some time with no reply. He was just about to cancel the call when it was finally answered.

'Crofts.'

Buller could hear he was out of breath and could also tell he was annoyed at being interrupted.

'What are you up to, Mr Happy?' he said cheerily.

'If you must know, I am currently searching through a manky flat in Hastings full of drugs and crap, with a dead druggie in the corner staring at me! What do you want?' Crofts barked.

Buller laughed. 'Sorry, mate, I should have guessed you were busy. You always pick the best places!' Crofts didn't reply, so Buller continued, 'I thought you'd like to know that I've just come from the Johnson trial.'

'Shit, I forgot about that,' Crofts answered, thawing slightly. 'How did it go?'

'Well, thanks to all my hard work and a little bit of help from you,' Buller said, laughing at his own little joke, 'he's got a life sentence.'

'Brilliant!' Crofts replied, and then passed the information to whoever he was with.

Buller heard a little cheer from the background and smiled to himself.

'I'm so glad,' Crofts said. 'That was a long old scene to do, and we only got the smallest bits of evidence, but that is all that is needed. Makes the job worthwhile.'

'I know,' replied Buller. 'You know I always like to take the mickey, but I must admit the forensic evidence on this job really was the final piece in that jigsaw that you're always on about.'

Crofts laughed. 'I know you do, but it just goes to show how close a call it is in some jobs. If the cleaners had used a bit more disinfectant in the sink or the shower, we wouldn't have got the traces of blood from there, and if we hadn't found a tiny smudge of blood under the edge of the bed, he might have got away with it.'

Buller smiled. 'If, indeed.'

THE END

A NOTE FROM THE PUBLISHER

Thank you for reading this book. If you enjoyed it please do consider leaving a review on Amazon to help others find it too.

We hate typos. All of our books have been rigorously edited and proofread, but sometimes mistakes do slip through. If you have spotted a typo, please do let us know and we can get it amended within hours.

info@bloodhoundbooks.com

Printed in Great Britain
by Amazon

18330367R00157